P9-DOF-965

ZIONS CAUSE

[1920–1950]

A NOVEL BY

JIM PEYTON

ALGONQUIN BOOKS OF CHAPEL HILL   1987

Published by
Algonquin Books of Chapel Hill
Post Office Box 2225
Chapel Hill, North Carolina 27515-2225

in association with
Taylor Publishing Company
1550 West Mockingbird Lane
Dallas, Texas 75235

Printed in the United States of America.

Library of Congress Cataloging-in-Publication Data
Peyton, Jim, 1926–
  Zions cause, (1920–1950).

  I. Title.
PS3566.E98Z35   1987   813'.54   86-20581
ISBN 0–912697–54–7

First Edition

Contents

Zions Cause
[1920]

They said it was August, and that's about right. It would have needed to be August if you wanted that many witnesses, because with little or nothing left to do in the fields, they would have been there on the store porch: Mr. Hayes with his chair tilted back against the wall and his hat brim along the bridge of his nose; the rest arranged around the porch floor out of the sun; and all overcome except Jr. Pease, who at nine years old could not keep still more than a minute and would have been jiggling about somewhere.

The dust must have been ankle-deep in the road, so that anyone looking could not have missed the swirl. And with all that heat, the air would have been still, the only sound maybe the slow wheeze of breathing, so that a blare of trumps, however distant, would have been clear had anyone been listening.

But they all missed it, even Jr. Pease: rider and mule and swirl of dust drifting along the road; and maybe somewhere trumps and tambourines and maybe even some sackbuts and psalteries too bringing them on.

They missed it, until Jr. Pease by chance jiggled around in the right directon and hollered. And Mr. Hayes looked along his hat brim and brought his chair legs down and bounced them all awake.

And I guess she missed it, too. From her room in the living quarters behind the store she would have had no view of the road; and even if the view had been hers to take, it is doubtful that she would have been enticed from that secret refuge of hers long enough to have noticed, or heard any blare or jangle, boom or twang there might have been to hear.

So he was almost on them when they saw him: that little mule belly deep in a swirl of dust, gliding along as if on wheels, and he astride in black frock coat and hat, white shirt and black string tie, and it the middle of August.

They marked his hands: big and red, like a split-open watermelon dangling out of each coat sleeve, somebody said; and his face: long and narrow, they said, as if there might have been some family connection between him and that little mule he was riding; and the cross: shiny but plain, hanging from his neck by a leather thong. But most of all, they marked his eyes, which under the deep shade of that wide hat brim seemed to have a light of their own. They burned, penetrated, some said convicted.

It looked as if he would pass them by, but directly in front of the store that little mule made a square turn, stepped out of that swirl of dust and stopped. And from under that hat brim those eyes raked the porch, touched upon every shrinking man and boy among them, froze Jr. Pease in midjiggle, and settled upon Mr. Hayes. And when it came, his voice had a hollow ring, as if, someone said, he was talking into a bucket. And he said to Mr. Hayes, "I come in the cause of Zion."

I guess, if they ever did, the trumps were blaring then, and the tambourines were jangling, and the sackbuts and psalteries booming and twanging.

Nobody remembered if Mr. Hayes answered, or if he did what it was. And if he remembered he ever afterward kept it to himself, as he kept to himself the straight of a lot of other matters. Mr. Hayes was a talkative man only on subjects of his own choosing. It left room for speculation, which is a sight more satisfying than fact and usually serves as well and sometimes maybe better.

Take the matter of money. What was verifiable was that the year he was eighteen both his parents, who could never quite manage to cope, contracted something or other and gave up and died. They had come over from the next county to sharecrop on somebody that year. He loaded them on a wagon and took them back to bury them and just kept going. Then two years later he showed up again with a wad of cash, which he used to buy that first piece of land and build the store and stock it, and with that sword and pair of pistols that were afterward to hang on the living room wall.

What was speculated, however, was that during those two years Mr. Hayes had been all the way to Cuba to fight Spaniards, had even run with Teddy Roosevelt up San Juan Hill and was made an officer for it in the field. And later he was put in charge of supplies, which he found out could be sold instead of just parceled out for nothing. It was said that for a while he ran it like a regular store and everything he took in clear profit, until they caught up with him and he got out just one jump ahead.

It might have been true. Mr. Hayes, while he never confirmed it, never denied it either.

It was surely true that somewhere in the back of his head, behind all that buying and building and stocking, there was the idea of empire. How else explain that sign? It went the whole width of the store, was meant to be read at a distance:

HAYESVILLE

IN OLD KENTUCKY

THE MOST OF THE BEST FOR THE LEAST

In time and under different circumstances Hayesville it might have become.

It must have been empire, still, and consequently heirs he had in mind when a year or so later he locked up and left and after a while brought back a wife. It must have been heirs; it was not looks. She was one of these big-boned, long-necked, awkward women, by all accounts full of gall and wormwood and, as it turned out, barren. But for better than fifteen years, he stuck by his bargain.

They used to call it consumption. It was as good a name as any, for they say it sucked her dry. When all that was left was bones and drum-tight skin, she sent away for Susan.

Susan was a niece or younger sister, depending on who was telling it, anyway close kin and reportedly all she had left. I found a photograph hidden away among his papers, faded and slightly out of focus, which I suppose fits.

She is seated in a chair by a window, her arms cradled over her breast and her feet tucked up beneath her. The view is full-face, but the light falls from the side so half is in shadow. Her head is tilted up slightly, her eyes downcast, her hair covers much of her shoulders and falls down over her arms and breast, dark in the picture, but they said the highlights were deep red and that in sunlight it was a glory to behold. Her figure is thin and long-boned, evidence of her kinship to Mrs. Hayes, but not ill-proportioned. That photograph was the only thing of hers he kept, and that hidden away, incongruous among his articles of empire.

Anyway, at the time Susan came the empire was his main obsession. And Mrs. Hayes, who had contributed nothing to it and who no longer had the strength to do for him or even for herself, could lie back and with a good conscience take her time in dying, which she did for more than a year and most of that bedfast. And Susan looked after her and after him and when he had to be out empiring, she even looked after the store.

They made it a point to come, especially at first. Let him leave and there they would be on some pretext or other, because they had to make up their minds about her.

There was a remoteness there, an air of inattention which frustrated them. They would find her behind the counter, but as if without purpose or design and seemingly oblivious to all about her. It was as if they and the store had not enough substance to fully register upon her senses. Consequently, when they spoke to her, to give their orders or to inquire about the condition of Mrs. Hayes, it would be in tones louder than normal in an effort to capture and hold her attention. And she would answer adequately but in as abbreviated a way as possible, and serve them as best she could, accepting silently their help in finding and pricing items. No one could remember her ever calling any of them by name.

They felt the slight but not personally, since no individual was singled out to bear more of the burden than another. Even those two or three who fancied themselves studs, and so were challenged by any fact of femaleness, did not feel explicitly rejected, not even ignored, only unnoticed. So the reaction was disappointment and regret rather than anger. Eventually, they made up their minds to it: Susan was peculiar. And having labeled it, they accepted it.

In time, they even developed a respect and something of an affection for her. However barred from full membership in their world, she managed somehow to cope with it. The quality of her housekeeping met their standards. Mr. Hayes was apparently well enough looked after. And they could only praise her treatment and tolerance of Mrs. Hayes, whose disposition in health had at best been difficult and in sickness had deteriorated. Maybe they even made personal use of her, sensing here the ideal confidant, balancing the possibility of inattention against the unlikelihood of breach of confidence.

So when in the end Mrs. Hayes turned against both of them, they couldn't credit it. Some of them had been there visiting; and as they were leaving, Mrs. Hayes, now barely able to whisper, beckoned them close.

"They can't wait," she told them. "They ain't even got the decency to wait until I'm dead and gone."

Then they said she was taken by a fit of coughing; and Susan, who had been there in the room all along, off somewhere out of the way, came to hold her up and wipe off the blood. And as they were slipping out the door, they said they could hear her saying it over to Susan. But they couldn't credit it.

It was not long after that Mrs. Hayes finally got around to dying and was duly laid to rest. Everybody looked to Susan to go back to wherever it was she came from. And when time passed and that didn't happen, they waited for Mr. Hayes to do the right thing. And when that didn't happen either, they shook their heads and tried to think the worst, but found they could not.

Well, they might think the worst of him but not of her. For they had not missed how a noise from the living quarters, a click of a dish or a thump of a door, almost too faint to register upon their awareness, would be enough to stop him in midsentence and set him over a space or two so that he never seemed to start back on the same track. Or the way his eyes would follow her when at his bidding she would come into the store to take over when he needed to be out.

Empire is a strong obsession. But he was in the grip of something stronger, something that would endure not only non-response but seemingly betrayal and certainly outrage.

The non-response they knew. And perhaps they also sensed that the nature of his passion was such that it would not allow him to violate innocence. Anyway, the arrangement, whatever it was, seemed to have been accepted without serious question.

And so Susan continued to keep his house and cook his meals and fill in when he went out—always at a distance. Then one day, out of a swirl of dust and straddling that little mule, whether with accompaniment or not, one came in the cause of Zion.

They did not tarry long, the witnesses to his coming. Perhaps the glare of those eyes was more than they at that time could endure. So as soon as pride or decency allowed, they slipped away. And early the next morning, when curiosity drove them back, they found Mr. Hayes, chair hitched around to the end of the porch, contemplating, they thought, the rear end of that little mule as it cropped the grass in the side yard of the store.

"Still here?" they asked. Mr. Hayes nodded in the direcaton of the locust thicket which bordered the side yard and the road. And then they could hear the chunk of the axe and the rustle of leaves as saplings fell.

"What's he doing?" they asked. But all Mr. Hayes knew was that his offer of a bed for the night had been accepted without thanks and that all his questions had brought forth only quotes of Scripture or what sounded like Scripture, none of which was particularly enlightening. The meals, night and morning, had been swallowed quickly and with apparent indifference; and he had left the breakfast table early, without apology or explanation, and had gone through the store and outside. Mr. Hayes, coming on later to the store porch, had heard the axe and had gone back and checked the stock and found one missing.

"It's high time I found out," Mr. Hayes said and stood up. Jr. Pease jiggled up and down a time or two and then found out he couldn't wait and went tearing aross the side yard and disappeared into the thicket. But before Mr. Hayes could make it to the edge of the porch, here Jr. Pease came backing out again as if somehow time had reversed itself and was now running in slow motion. And then here came the back of that black frock coat and that wide-brimmed hat and finally those watermelon hands dragging a couple of eight-inch-thick locust posts about ten feet long.

They watched, frozen, as clearing the thicket he shouldered those poles and, straining under the load, swung around and step by step made his slow way to the middle of the yard (each step matched by Jr. Pease except in reverse), where he stopped, head down, back and knees bent by that weight sloping across his shoulder, that black frock coat hanging like a cape, and stood there a long moment before finally letting those poles slide to the ground.

Then Mr. Hayes stepped from the porch and crossed the yard, the others following. "Now just what would them be for?" he asked.

He straightened up, slowly and deliberately, those eyes touching them all before they finally fixed on Mr. Hayes. "And Abraham builded him an altar unto the Lord," he said.

It took some time before they finally understood that what he had in mind was not an altar but a brush arbor.

Mr. Hayes asked their question for them. "For what?"

"To hold the meeting in," he told them.

They helped build it, going home for tools, those that lived close enough, working without direction while Mr. Hayes watched from his chair on the porch.

They built it in the yard beside the store, cutting what they needed out of that locust thicket, shooing that little mule out of the way so they could sink the holes for the roof supports, nailing on lintels and laying a latticework of saplings across them. They finished it in midafternoon and were drifting over to the store porch to join Mr. Hayes when that bucket voice stopped them.

"For lo, Jacob wrestled with the angel of the Lord," he said, "and so must I."

They watched him cross the yard to the edge of the thicket where he turned and said, "We will commence at sundown."

Then he disappeared into the thicket and they followed his progress by ear, the rustling diminishing as he went on, until when they thought he had passed beyond earshot the rustling and thrashing came on loud again, then cut off sharply.

Mr. Hayes brought his chair legs down and jarred them to life again. "Let that be a lesson to you, boys," he said. "Don't go messing around with no angels."

Then that bucket voice started, low at first, then louder, rising and falling in a regular rhythm, building to a bawl or a bellow where it would be joined by a thrash or two before dropping down again.

Nobody remarked on it, but they found they could not carry on with anything else. Nor could they seem to find a comfortable place on the porch but kept shifting and swapping. So after a while they made excuses and left, until Jr. Pease, who as always was the last, finally said it: "I ain't going to stand here earsdropping no more neither."

They did not wait for dark. The sun was only level with the roof of that fresh-built brush arbor when the first load pulled in. Before sunset they were all there, the Theobolds, the Posers, the Bumpuses, the Heddins, the Blackburns and the Gustos, who were the last, clattering up in that big touring car that Mr. Billy had bought two years before, the only one then like it in that part of the country, in a cloud of dust with those girls hanging over the sides of the back seat and Mrs. Gusto in front, high nosed, holding on to the windshield with one hand

and to her hat with the other. That hat, they claimed, was about the size of a washtub and needed to be.

They settled themselves under the brush arbor, the women with their fans going, clucking softly to each other like chickens come to roost and settling in for the night. Some of the men had lifted Mrs. Blackburn, chair and all, out of their wagon and carried her up to the front. She had been paralyzed by a stroke years ago, but it never affected her appetite, so she made quite a load. Others hung the lanterns from the wagons on those locust uprights.

The thicket was silent now, so they judged he was at supper. After a while Mr. Hayes came out to the store porch and hitched his chair around in their directon and sat picking his teeth. And then later, they saw Susan come out the back door and throw out the dishwater. And still they thought he was inside. So the rustle from the thicket took them by surprise.

In the gathering shadows, he was hard to make out. At first they saw only a patch of white floating toward them, which turned out to be that boiled shirt. Then they could pick out the rest: that black frock coat was now wrinkled and dusty with a rip in one sleeve; both knees of his trousers were caked with dirt; one side of the button-on collar of that boiled shirt had sprung loose and was flapping; and, when he was on them, they could see that the backs of those big hands were crosshatched with scratches and the knuckles raw. And no doubt some found themselves reflecting on angels, even some who ought to have known better.

He went to the front and stood behind that locust stump they had set for the pulpit.

"And the Lord said, let there be light," he said.

But he had to say it again before they realized what he wanted and got up and lit the lanterns and brought one and set it on the pulpit.

They could not have done better or worse, depending on how you look at it. Lit from below, with shadows blacking out nose and eyesockets and the hollows of his cheeks and the rest colored by lantern light, that long narrow face must have looked like a fresh skull, or as some said, what they imagined Rawhead or Bloodybones to look like in the story they used to tell to terrify the little ones.

So they would have been receptive to his text: that the wages of sin is death.

I say text, but it was not that, not a framework for coherent argument, but what he threw in here and there as it suited him or perhaps according to his own design; because he was not concerned with, maybe not even capable of, coherence, and certainly had no need to be, since it was not minds he was after.

It started as it had in the thicket, low and slow, building as it went on: that hollow voice rising and falling and picking up speed; those eyes deep in their black sockets flashing in the light; those big hands weaving and waving and slashing the air. It was all a tangle of Scripture or near Scripture and lines of hymns and *yes Jesuses* and *hear me Lords* and then that text shouted out and hammered in with one of those big hands smashing into the pulpit or plank bench or locust upright, whichever happened to be nearest.

After a while, it moved them: what started out as a toe tap and a whisper before long turned into a knee bounce and a loud *yes Jesus!*—until finally that was not enough for some so they had to get up and out and go to the front where there would be room enough to jerk and shout and if need be jump around.

And when he changed it, he must not have missed a beat, switching from sin and death to the gift of God and everlasting life, that hollow voice bawling and bellowing it out and those big hands, bruised now and bloody, smacking into whatever was handy. And that brought more of them to the front, jumping and shouting and keeping time, so that they filled and jammed the space in front of the pulpit. So when Luster Pease was overcome with ecstasy, several next to him were struck and someone staggered and fell against Mrs. Blackburn, upsetting her chair and leaving her flat of her back and squealing on the ground.

That stopped him and so stopped them. The only sound left was Mrs. Blackburn grunting as she tried to sit up, and when she finally made it, that stopped too.

Taking the lantern from the pulpit, he moved over to her, holding it high as he stood looking down at her. She was sitting there with her fat legs stuck out and her mouth hanging open, unconcerned, probably unaware, that her skirt was hiked up over her knees, staring up at that cross on his chest somebody said like a bird charmed by a snake.

He reached down, taking his time, and laid a hand on her head and spoke in a low voice.

"Take up thy bed and walk."

And when she did not move, he said it again, louder. And when she still did not move, that big hand clamped around her head and he yelled it.

"In the name of God, woman, get up and walk like I told you!"

And she did: first rolling over to her hands and knees and

then slowly, pushing and grunting, she began to rise. Someone started in to help her but one of those big hands swung out and stopped him. She made it alone and stood there before them on legs that had not carried her in fifteen years, swaying some but erect.

But that was not enough for him.

"Walk," he told her. "Walk!"

With her eyes fastened on him, she put one foot out and eased her weight on it. Then the other. Then it all broke loose again, with everybody crowding to the front, laughing and crying and jumping up and down, and some climbing up on the benches to get a good look at Mrs. Blackburn parading back and forth in front of the pulpit now and squealing every step. Luster Pease was overcome again, but they gave him room this time. Mrs. Gusto forgot herself and joined in, one hand hanging on to that hat and the other waving in the air. Jr. Pease, they said, skinned up one of those roof supports and hung there watching his daddy. And somebody claimed even that little mule wandered over and stuck his head in to watch.

So it was understandable that they did not see him go. I doubt even Mr. Hayes noticed from his chair there at the edge of the store porch; his attention would have been on Mrs. Blackburn and the miracle, with maybe the idea already gathering in his head.

When they finally missed him, and that took some time because it had to run down, they were not greatly concerned, maybe not even surprised, because they sensed a gulf between him and them. He had gone to the house or maybe to the thicket again, wherever it was to be alone or with company more suitable.

As they were leaving, drifting past Mr. Hayes on the store porch, he leaned out and spoke to Mrs. Blackburn, supported now by a son on either side but still on her feet and walking.

"He actually done that?" he asked her.

"I could feel it coming out of his hand through my head and right down into my legs," she told him. "I could feel the power and I just upped and walked."

They said Mr. Hayes didn't say any more, just sat back and looked at her until after a while they led her on to the wagon.

The next day they didn't congregate at the store. But in the course of running all over the place trying to find somebody who didn't know to tell it to, they would pass by, and now and then one or another would stop and inquire as to his whereabouts.

"Not seen him since breakfast," Mr. Hayes would tell them. "For all I know he's out yonder in that thicket somewheres with a hammerlock on an angel or it with one on him."

By six o'clock the results of their running around began to show up, some of them from as far as ten and fifteen miles away, on horses and in buggies and wagons with chairs set up for the old and infirm and one even with an old woman completely bedridden on a pallet in the back. Before sunset the benches were all filled and all the chairs from the wagons; that old woman's pallet was laid out in front of the pulpit and one of her kin sitting beside her with a fan going; every one of those locust uprights had two or three hanging on it; and there were still several left milling around without places. After a while somebody must have got concerned about that old woman getting stepped on and backed a wagon up to the edge of that brush arbor and laid her in it and took out the tailgate so she could see. Then some of the others brought their wagons up close, and those left out found places on them.

He came out of the darkness up to the pulpit and without preamble began to preach. It took some time to work them up because maybe they had their minds on miracles, but eventually it happened and they began to stream to the front, dancing and jiggling and whooping. And when he stepped around the pulpit, someone took up the lantern and lighted his way to the chairs where he listened to each complaint and then placed that big hand on each head and gave his commandment; and pain eased, vigor was restored, and one knotty arthritic leaped from his chair and went dancing around the pulpit. He turned then to that old woman in the wagon, the sweat running down his face now, and reached out and touched her and spoke as if to a malingerer.

"Get up from there!"

She made it to her elbows, pushing against that hand with her head, then sat up, and finally swung herself around so that her legs were hanging off the end of that wagon. And then she stopped.

"Get up, I say!"

Mr. Hayes had come from the store porch and through that crowd and nobody had noticed him until he spoke.

"Wait," he said.

That big hand drew back from the woman and he turned, taking his time, his face all in shadow now, except some claimed they could see his eyes and that cross shining in the dark.

"Can you cast out devils?" Mr. Hayes asked.

"What?"

"Can you heal minds too?"

His answer was a long time coming and then so low that with all the whooping and hollering going on they missed it, those who were close and listening. Whatever it was it must have satisfied, because Mr. Hayes took him by the arm and led him off into the dark in the direction of the house.

It must have been near midnight when they began to run down and those buggies and wagons began to load up and move off. The wagon with that old woman in it left with her lying down on that pallet, but she claimed she could sit up now any time she felt like it. Some of them coming by the store saw Mr. Hayes there, on the porch in the dark, his chair tilted back against the wall. They said he neither spoke nor even seemed to notice them. And no wonder. For the passion would have been strong again, rekindled by the hope that sprang from seeing the lame walk and the weak made strong.

What happened that night had to be speculated. Mr. Hayes must have taken him on into Susan's room. And late as it was, she would already have been in bed. Mr. Hayes may have offered her a word of explanation, but whether he did or not, it would not have been like her to question or object.

It is hard to understand why Mr. Hayes would leave them alone. Maybe earsdropping, as Jr. Pease had called it, even where his own interest was concerned, made him uncomfortable. Or maybe he was asked to leave, the request made indirectly through some phrase or paraphrase of Scripture so he would have had to puzzle it out. Whatever the reason, Mr. Hayes left and waited on the store porch, while in her room, sitting on the edge of the bed maybe, he reached out and touched her with those big hands and did whatever else that was done. And she would have endured it without objection, perhaps without apparent awareness, for such was her way.

How long it went on, how long Mr. Hayes sat in that chair on the store porch before he went in to see about them must be speculated too. What is known is that the next day he and that little mule were gone, never to return again, and that in Susan there was no apparent change.

There was disappointment at first, bordering on anger, but that soon changed to relief because they somehow sensed that they could not too long take a diet that rich.

Mr. Hayes seemed to bear up and in a few days was close to being himself again. So when the idea evolved, and no one knows who thought of it, he went along. He even donated the land.

They built the church down the road a ways but still within sight of the store. They built it themselves out of what they had. It was not imposing, but it did have a small steeple marking it as a place of worship. They named it Zions Cause.

The dedication service, which came on the first day of winter, was an all-day affair with a basket dinner. Pastors of churches in neighboring counties showed up and preached. Mrs. Blackburn walked down the aisle stepping high so all could witness her triumph. That old arthritic was using a cane but he was still moving. They even brought in that old woman on that pallet and she showed them how she could sit up. Others testified how they were cured or eased. Luster Pease was overcome again. It was a great event.

Mr. Hayes did not attend nor, of course, did Susan. Shortly

before the dedication he had become uncommunicative, withdrawn, sometimes even savage when they pressed him too hard.

A month later they knew why. Susan was with child.

They could not really believe it was Mr. Hayes', but the alternative was even harder to believe. And no one, not even Mrs. Gusto who broached it, could seriously entertain the idea of immaculate conception.

It was a hard birth. Susan did not survive it, but the baby did. And as soon as they saw him, they were in no doubt as to who the father was. The physical resemblance was unmistakable.

A Little Honey
[1923]

No one ever knew how he came by the idea, not even Will himself. He told how he was at the breakfast table and it came to him. He said he was just looking over his mind that morning and there it was. So he said he spoke along the table to his boys and told them: "I'm thinking about digging me a well."

Will certainly had no need for a well because not thirty steps from his back door was the best spring in the country, never known to go dry. Everybody said he was crazy. Well, maybe he was.

I recall a sermon I heard years ago about honey. The preacher, whoever it was, taking a little liberty with the text, told how when Jacob was sending to Egypt to buy feed because they had had a bad year, he said to his boys: "Boys, take a little honey along. It will make things so much sweeter on the way." That thought has stuck with me through the years. Maybe it explains something here, I don't know.

Anyway, there had never been much honey in Will's life. Old man Poser was a sharecropper, and as I heard it—because

this was before my time, you see—raised little or nothing but
younguns and hell on whatever place he happened to be that
year. Will was the oldest, and they said the old man was hard
on him. Let something not go to suit him, and they said he
would take to Will with a leather plowline and stripe him until
sometimes the blood would come through his shirt. And Will
would take it, they said, and never open his mouth or let on
that he thought he was being mistreated. And that went on until Will got to be good-sized, maybe fifteen or sixteen years
old. And then one day old man Poser got on one of his ram-
pages and came at Will with that leather plowline, and they
told how Will took it away from him—snatched it out of his
hand and he hitting at Will with it all the time—and whipped
him until he couldn't walk. They said old man Poser had to
crawl on hands and knees all the way from the barn, where
Will took to him with that leather, to the house so he could get
the cuts on his back and legs fixed up. And Will, they said,
went straight and hired out to Mr. Billy Gusto, who was glad to
get him, as I guess any man might have been who had three
hundred acres and a house full of younguns and not a boy in
the bunch. And a few days later old man Poser left the country
on a pile of quilts in the bed of a wagon with younguns and
belongings stacked around him and Mrs. Poser on the seat
handling their bone-poor mismatched team, with not as much
as a by-your-leave to whoever it was who was their then
landlord.

It must have been some easier on Will at the Gustos, but
still not what you would call a bed of roses. For one thing,
there were those three hundred acres and just Will and Mr.
Billy, and Mr. Billy was the type of man who thought himself

better at directing than doing. And for another, there was Mrs. Gusto, who was born and bred in Virginia and was satisfied that she had married beneath her; she arranged for Will to sleep in the barn in the harness room and take his meals in the kitchen after the family had finished. Then too, Mr. Billy—and in that day and time most would have agreed with him—considered board and keep wages aplenty for a fifteen- or sixteen-year-old that had no other place to go. Easier maybe, but no bed of roses.

Meanwhile, there were those girls growing up for Mr. Billy and that wife of his to find places for. The oldest were twins, Essie and Bessie, and about as much alike as summer and winter. Essie was the one who kept the parlor full. I suppose every free man in riding distance at one time or another hung his hat in Mr. Billy's front hall and set his feet on Mrs. Gusto's parlor floor. But not Will. Whatever he felt, whatever it was that stood him outside that parlor window every night to watch what went on inside, he knew his place. And if he didn't, there was Mrs. Gusto who did. After a while Essie picked the finest John B. Stetson she could find on those hall hat pegs and left with it, and then Will didn't have to stand out in the cold anymore. And not long after that, the next one, Evaline I think, began eyeing those hat pegs and made her choice. And Bessie was left standing without as much as a dollar straw and not even a hope for one. And then, I guess, Mr. Billy took that wife of his into that parlor of hers and shut the door, and after a while came out and went down to the harness room and shut that door too, maybe, because the next anybody knew, Will was building a house in the middle of forty acres of what had been Mr. Billy's land for him and that cross-eyed and crooked-toothed Bessie to live in.

It is my doubt that Will had a say as to where on that forty-acre sassafras-bushed and gully-washed tract he would build that house; because it is my belief that Will, or any man who was locating the place where he expected to abide his life-time, would not of his own choosing select a spot in the middle of what was to become cultivated field, that far from the road, and not a tree in sight to give it shade. It must have been Mr. Billy who set the site there, because that was where the spring was, so there wouldn't have been the trouble and ex-pense of sinking a well. And that house, too, must have been Mr. Billy's design—square, like a box maybe or like a barn, and not even as much as a porch, where a man might get out of the sun or where in the evening after supper he might sit and rest and maybe watch the dark fall and maybe, as the saying is, invite his soul; no, not even a tree where a bird might sing and which in the day might cast a shade on that tin roof; and not even a front yard where a flower might grow, because that was to become cultivated field and a man couldn't in that day and time take from his field to make a place for flowers, not in good conscience.

But time went sliding along like a river, sometimes slow, sometimes fast, and sometimes even seeming to flow back-wards; and sassafras bushes and gullies turned into clean, smooth fields; and every year there was another one to fill a place at the breakfast table, maybe cross-eyed or crooked-toothed, but sound of limb and strong, so that one day forty acres would not be enough to contain—much less exercise—

them all; until sixteen years, about, from the time Mr. Billy took Mrs. Gusto into that parlor and shut the door; and twenty years, about, from the time Will took that leather to old man Poser; and thirty-six years, about, from the time Mrs. Poser birthed him in whatever bedbug- and rat-plagued sharecropper shack it happened to be—Will, sitting at the breakfast table, looked over his mind and found it there, already familiar, planted, sprouted, growing there maybe from the first. And he walked out his front door ten steps into his cornfield where he marked a cross in the ground with the side of his shoe and said to his sons coming out the door to follow him, speaking maybe in a manner solemn and ceremonial, in a tone seasoned by sixteen or twenty or thirty-six years of honeyless existence, and assuming maybe an unconscious dignity standing there surrounded by sons and shoulder-high corn and pointing to the cross scratched in the crusted earth: "Here's where I dig my well."

It came at a good time, too; in season, you might say, since with the crops laid by everybody was left with too much time on their hands. Will was in town every day, and some days two or three times, in and out of Big Jack Heddin's blacksmith shop, with a paper under his arm, rolled up and covered with designs, and they drawn by Herman, Will's next-to-oldest, on brown wrapping paper from Mr. Hayes' store while Will stood over him, accepting or rejecting, knowing which he wanted though he himself could not make them, directing the boy who at fourteen years old already could. And the forge was going every day, so everybody didn't have to sit around just passing time but could go and watch the sparks flying from the anvil where Big Jack was working iron bars to fit the designs on

Will's paper. And they could go out to Will's place, walk through his cornfield to get there, and watch the dirt come flying out of that hole, flung by some one of Will's sons, the hole soon too deep for him to be visible; and later, when the hole was even deeper, watch it being drawn out by bucket. And they could watch the well-house being raised, with its pyramid roof whose four combs were swirled and curlicued with wrought iron, and the pillars which supported it wrought iron, too, and swirled and curlicued. And then they could talk about how a man was crazy who would build in front of his house and in the edge of his cornfield a well-house (and not just that, not satisfied with that, but one that put his house and everything in it, and everything in theirs, too, to shame) overtopping a well that was not yet complete, was in fact just started, with no assurance or indication that it would be anything but dry, which he didn't need, had no imaginable use for in the first place. But Will went right along, measuring and fitting and directing, as if he was maybe blind to that crowd around the door of Big Jack's blacksmith shop, and that other crowd milling around in his field and breaking down his already jointed corn was maybe invisible; as if he was deaf to Jr. Pease hollering, "What is it, Will, a privy for the Queen of Sheba?" and couldn't hear them laughing that thought it was funny every time; until finally that fancy well-house was finished and the windlass working, and there was nothing left to do but watch a bucket of dirt coming out of that hole now and then and maybe every couple of hours one of Will's boys coming up and another going down to take his place.

It was hot because it was getting on toward August, so they that had to stand in the field were suffering somewhat because

that shoulder-high corn blocked off any breeze that might have
been blowing. Jr. Pease had shortened it to "What is it, Will?"
but they could still laugh because after two weeks they knew
the rest of it. Will, still blind, still deaf, had nothing to do now
but stand by that hole, shaded by that swirled- and curlicued-
combed roof of that fancy well-house, and watch the dirt coming out by the slow and steady bucketful. The morning passed
and some were talking about going home for a bite when Will
told whichever one it was to quit and come up. So most of
them were leaving, scattering through the cornfield, so that
when Jr. Pease hollered again, it must have sounded to Will, if
he was listening, as if not only his neighbors but his cornfield,
too, was laughing at him. Only a few were there to see Will set
his foot in the bucket and order his boys to let him down; and
they must have thought he was going to see about the depth or
the plumb or the workmanship, so they left, too. But in the
middle of the afternoon when they came drifting back and
found not only Will's sons ringing that hole but Bessie, too,
whom they had not seen during those two weeks or heard or
even thought of, with her hands rolled into her apron and staring maybe into the hole, at least her head was inclined that
way, they knew they had missed something. And when they
heard her, in that whiny way she had, saying, "Will? Will,
honey? You come on out now, you hear? You come on out now
and eat," they asked one another, *"Still there? Been there all
this time? You mean to stand there and tell me that all the time
we've been gone he has been in that hole? Why, what on earth?
What on earth could he be doing in there?"*

Then they were no longer satisfied to stand out in the cornfield but shoved up as close as they could get, as many as could under the roof of that fancy well-house, and stood tip-toe, stretching their necks, trying to see in a curve over the heads of the ones in front and down into the hole, and cocked their heads and cupped their hands to their ears to hear Bessie whining, "Will? You come on out now, you hear me? Will?" And then the silence was long and unfulfilling, as when you drop a rock into a hole but never hear it hit bottom, until finally the tail of that crowd said, *"What did he say?"* and the head said, *"Nothing."*

"Well, can't nobody see him?" the tail said. *"Can't nobody tell what he's doing?"*

And one of those boys at the edge said, "Nothing. He ain't doing nothing."

So the river was slow, too slow for them ringing the edge of that hole and for them shoved up under that fancy roof and for them that couldn't even get that close but had to stand in the cornfield in the sun. The heat was parching, but nobody could go to the spring for water: not anybody under the roof lest they lose their place, and not anybody in the sun lest they miss the chance of taking the place of somebody under the roof who did. So because there was nothing else to do it with, they had to fill that particular slice of time with tedium and thirst.

It was not until the sun was lying along the top of that shoulder-high corn, and they who had endured so long had begun maybe to wonder if it was never going to be over and done with, that there was a stir among them at the edge of that hole. One of those boys bent over and said something, and another jumped up and began to crank the windlass. Then those ouside the well-house tried to get inside, and those inside tried to get closer to the edge, so that for a while it was doubtful whether they would not all be swallowed by the hole. Will came up blinking at the light and was helped out by some one of those boys. For a minute time stopped because that crowd had to have time to draw in its breath, and then it, head and tail together now, hollered, *"Will! What on earth was you doing in there?"*

Then time stopped again while Will looked at that crowd as if for the first time; and then he said, "Nothing," and turned and went into the house, Bessie and those boys behind him.

"Nothing!" Mr. Hayes said when they who had been there came to the store that night and told him. "Nothing! You mean he sat there in that hole half the day and then claimed to be doing nothing? And you stood there in the sun that long here in the middle of summer to wait on a man to get through doing nothing? Well, if the Fool Killer comes around, I advise you to hide, because he sure won't be looking for Will Poser!"

But they were all there that next morning and Mr. Hayes, too, because the store wouldn't be doing any business since all the business was in Will's cornfield. And Will was at the edge of that hole, blind again and deaf, and one of those boys was at the windlass and another one down there sending up dirt. The river was slow and steady, and, if that crowd wanted excitement, it looked as if it was going to have to get along on leftovers. But at midmorning Will sent down another one of those boys without bringing the first one up, and soon it was taking two to handle the windlass and another to empty the spare bucket. So the crowd said, *"Wait,"* because the river was reaching the narrows and it was getting hard to keep up. And then, a little later, when Will himself went down—and that made three of them down there sending up dirt, so those left on top had to trot to keep up—the crowd hollered, *"Wait!"* because it had not yet puzzled out how there could be room for two in that hole, much less three. And still later, when the dirt was coming even faster, the crowd, surfeiting, hollered, *"Wait! Wait!"* but they would not—neither those below nor those above at the windlass and buckets—either because going that fast they couldn't hear or because caught up in the rush and swirl and swept along they could not. And when it got too fast for those at the windlass and buckets, the head of that crowd had to pitch in and help, some cranking and some running dirt, which made it too much for the tail, which had to get along on just watching, so that it despaired and hollered, *"Hey! Wait! How much deeper?"*

And Mr. Hayes, spinning the windlass, himself beginning to catch up, hollered back over his shoulder, "Not deeper! No, not deeper! Wider!"

That's right, wider. No sign, no promise yet of water, the dirt still coming out of that hole dry and crumbly, but Will was not going deeper, just wider, digging not down but out, as if he expected to strike a stream in the walls, and that crowd and Mr. Hayes, too, party to whatever folly was being perpetrated, caught up in the swirl and rush—the spinning windlass and the plunge and upsurge of buckets, the violent upheaval of dirt and the frenzied shuttle of them emptying—like trash in a cloudburst. And Bessie—coming at noon to stand with her hands in her apron and whine down, "Will? You come on and eat now, you hear me, Will?"—was caught as well, was handed a bucket by someone who hollered, "Run! Quick!" and so was swept up and carried along. It was not until the middle of the afternoon that Mr. Hayes, who was way ahead of everybody, finally caught up, stopped the windlass and so stopped everything else, and asked why. *"Why what?"* the crowd hollered, because it still hadn't had time.

"Why wider and not deeper," Mr. Hayes said. "Hey, Will, why are you going wider?"

The hole rumbled and the crowd said, *"What did he say?"*

"He said he needed the room," Mr. Hayes told them.

So they were caught, those who had intended only to be onlookers, trapped and taken and outraged, because maybe the nature of things will not allow an onlooker; maybe it is so fixed and appointed that those who share a particular slice of space and time must also share whatever guilt or triumph it works; for the well, itself without need or warrant and topped by that vain and wondrous well-house, was not to be a well at all but a room thirty feet below ground.

"What in creation for?" Mr. Hayes hollered, but the hole didn't rumble again. So they had to wait, Mr. Hayes and the rest, until it was finished, and then it had to come to them one at a time, because it was not something to be spoken, passed on.

Mr. Hayes was the first, because maybe it bothered him more than it did the others. He told how when he was going through the cornfield he met those boys out there trying to straighten up some of that trampled-down corn and asked where Will was.

"In the well," one of them told him.

"Well, what's he doing in there?" he asked.

"Sitting," another one said.

And the least one, Odie, said, "He's got him a chair down there."

Mr. Hayes said it was so. He said he looked over that low curbing that Will had since laid, and there was that hole all plastered as slick as a wall and maybe eight feet across at the bottom and Will in the middle in a rocking chair. Mr. Hayes said he never had a chance to ask his question, because Will looked up and saw him and touched a string down there somewhere that rang a little bell fixed on that well-house, and here came Bessie running, as he guessed Will had ordered her to do. "Send down another chair," he said Will told her, "and then get the boys and let Mr. Hayes down."

Mr. Hayes said that for a few minutes it wasn't anything, just cool and quiet and dark; and then he said he began to feel it: both of them sitting there not saying a word, and it began to come over him.

"It beat anything I ever saw," he said. "It was maybe like death, if death is, as it says somewhere, a place of utter peace, where the wicked cease from troubling and the weary be at rest. No, that was not really it at all. There was peace, all right, but not the peace of laying it down, surrendering. No, it was the peace of taking it up, taking it all up, everything, and being a part of it, being at one with it, the peace of knowing it all and understanding it and accepting it. It was like being God!"

But they had to find it out, each for himself, because

Mr. Hayes had still not said it right. Besides, it was never the same, changing from man to man. So one by one they went, wearing a path through Will's cornfield, to sit an hour or two, and some half the day, and then at the tinkle of that little bell to come up, wide-eyed and blinking, as if they had been asleep. And none could tell what it was.

And I don't know either. But then again, maybe I do. I keep thinking about that sermon I heard years ago. And I think that, whatever else was in that well, there was a little honey, too.

The Outrage
[1925]

Maybe Ish Theobold's trouble was that he was born little, outraged forty years by having to look up to everybody, to Mrs. Theobold, even to that ten-year-old boy of his.

So maybe that was why he chose Big Jack Heddin that time, who could drop a mule with his bare fist, taking up some mild joke that Big Jack was only rumored to have made on Mrs. Theobold's size—which whether he did or not was certainly true and obvious to everyone, Ish most of all—coming to stand in the road between Mr. Hayes' store and Big Jack's blacksmith shop, where everyone would have to witness it, and calling for Big Jack to come out; flinging aside Mrs. Theobold who had followed, not looking, only throwing out his hand as if to brush a fly, the back of it cracking across her face so that it sounded to us on the store porch like a breaking twig, saying, "Get away, woman. Get on back like I told you," and to Big Jack, standing in the door now and watching, too, with a look on his face not of alarm or anxiety, not even of surprise, but just plain unbelief, saying, "Now, come on, damn you. Come on and fight me!"—speaking past a throatful of gorge that squeezed his words into a hiss—"Come on, or must I come after you!"

But we on the store porch could not laugh, not because we didn't see the absurdity, but because we couldn't believe it, either. And when Big Jack stepped from the door, covering in just three strides the distance between the blacksmith shop and the middle of the road, standing half again as tall and measuring as much through the thigh as Ish did through the waist, it was even harder to believe. Big Jack, bending over and speaking in a tone so low that we had to strain to hear, asked, "What is it, Ish, what you got against me?" And Ish, squeezing past his choke and loud enough to be heard all the way out to Posers, hollered, "Insult me and mine, will you?" And Big Jack again, "Now wait a minute, Ish." And Ish, "I don't take that off nobody!" And then Ish was swinging, the licks sounding like apples falling in a windstorm, only he wasn't hitting anything but Big Jack's arm where Big Jack had it braced against his chest; and Big Jack was talking to him, low and easy, as if it might have been a skittish mare someone had brought him to shoe: "Ho, Ish. Easy now, Ish. Ho, boy." And Ish, looking like the spokes in a buggy wheel and sounding like apples in a windstorm, was hollering, "Not nobody! Not nothing nor nobody!"

Maybe Big Jack got tired. Or maybe he understood there was nothing else to do. Maybe knowing Ish he knew that nothing less would stop or satisfy him. Anyway, when it came, it was slow as if time had just about run down, and we could watch it from the beginning—coming from where it hung at his side and making into a fist on the way, slow, as if it were having to pull through water, and taking Ish just under the chin and lifting him, still slow, up and over, so we could see his eyes already turning back in his head and only the whites showing as he passed us on the way down. But we on the porch still could not laugh because not only could we see the absurdity, now we could believe it. And then time finally ran down, the last stroke was Ish hitting the dust, leaving Big Jack with his fist in the air and Mrs. Theobold with her mouth open and empty, as if we might have been looking at a picture in a stereopticon.

And when it started again, I guess out at the Posers a half a mile away they could hear Mrs. Theobold hollering, "Good Lord, you've killed him! Good Lord!" Then Big Jack could bring his fist down, and we could all go and see if it was so. But before we could get there, Big Jack had already picked him up out of the dust, over-gentle and clumsy, as a man handles a baby, and was carrying him into the blacksmith shop, with Mrs. Theobold following, her face red-marked where Ish had hit her, still hollering, "Good Lord, he's dead! Good Lord!"

But crowding around the door, trying to see in out of the sun, we could hear that he wasn't. Big Jack was giving him water, dipping it by the handfuls out of the shrinking vat and splashing it in his face, and we could hear Ish: "Hell fire, Jack, ain't you satisfied with just knocking my head off? Have you got to drown me, too?"

So it was over. But not ended. Because, you see, it was not Big Jack at all; it was the outrage. It showed in the way he cultivated his land—guiding his mule down the rows with that savage intensity, stabbing the double-shovel or scratch-harrow or whatever tool he was using at the roots of any grass or weed reckless enough to grow in his field, stopping the mule with a violent back-jerk of the lines to snatch out and fling down and grind under his heel some weed that the plow or harrow had failed to uproot or turn under, so that Mr. Hayes, who had fought Spaniards in Cuba, watching him pass the store in the morning with his wagon loaded with whatever tools he would be using that day, would say, "There he goes, boys, caisson and all, off to the wars again."

You could see it, too, in the way he fished: not with a pole and line and bait; no, just hands. He would go into the water and take them with his bare hands, hollering at us on the bank watching, "Do you think that a fish or anything else is better than a man, so that a man has got to set on the bank like he's afraid and trick it with a pole and line?"

This would be at the creek where it cut along that little piece of bottom ground where he raised corn nearly twice as tall as he was. We would be there watching, any of us who could take or make time, and we all usually did one or the other, and that ten-year-old boy that had already outgrown him, too. Ish would take off his clothes—no, rip them off, jerking and cursing buttons and straps—and fling them aside, shirt in one direction and overalls in another and underwear maybe someplace else, for that boy to gather up and straighten out. And then he would slide down the bank into the water, his arms and legs looking like those tree roots the creek had exposed in the bank, crooked and knotty and white like fresh-peeled hickory except the red of his hands and forearms where the sun had burned him. The water would be muddy and stagnant, opaque and covered with a green scum. He would work up and down the bank, all covered except his head—and it, severed by the water, alone and accusing, like John the Baptist only without a beard—feeling under the bank where the water had cut out a shelf. Then suddenly his head would jerk, bob like a cork on a line, maybe go completely under and then emerge again. And then it wouldn't be a head we would be looking at, it would be a hand, upraised as if in a gesture of triumph, holding by the gills a catfish—and it slapping the water and the arm, too, with its tail—which he would throw out to that boy to clean. And maybe the next time it wouldn't be a fish but a mud turtle he would throw out, mad and snapping, and we, shying and dodging out of its way, and he would holler, "Take and beat its head in, boy, before they hurt theirselves running over one another!"

But the day he met *it*, we were not there. The first we knew was when that wagon came flying down the road in the middle of the afternoon with just that boy in it, standing up and flailing at the mules with the ends of the lines like a Roman charioteer, and laying down a cloud of dust that blurred out everything he had already passed. As he passed the store, in that brief instant when we had him in profile before the dust caught up and blurred him out, too, we could see him leaning forward and his legs pumping, as if he might at any time run down the wagon tongue and leave mules and all behind; and we could see his mouth working, though we couldn't hear a sound, but whether because of the noise of the mules and wagon or, as Mr. Hayes said later, going that fast he had outrun his voice, was uncertain. And then we couldn't see anything but dust, but we could hear right away that the wagon had stopped, and we could hear Mrs. Theobold hollering, "Good Lord!"

Then the dust began to thin out, and we could see that boy taking the tailgate out of the wagon and Mrs. Theobold lifting Ish out, shouldering him like a sack of feed, and the boy following, still carrying the tailgate, which he had forgotten to put down. And we could hear the mules blowing and see their sides heaving, streaked dark with dust and sweat, and hear Mrs. Theobold in the house still going, "Good Lord!"

We had all got up and come to the edge of the store porch to watch, except Jr. Pease, who had gone to the middle of the road, and now we turned and looked at one another. Mr. Hayes started to speak, but just then that boy came out with the tailgate and put it back in the wagon and took out the mules and led them off to the barn, so he waited until that was done. Then he said, "You don't reckon one of them weeds snuck up behind him and cold-cocked him, do you?"

But we had to wait to find out until that boy had unharnessed and turned out the mules and come back through the house to look at Ish and then on to the store and told it, hollering some because maybe the trip was too fast and he wasn't quite through it yet.

"It sounded just like one of them trees had fell in the creek. We stopped the mules and run over to see what it was and got there just in time, too, because it was clear out of the water. Just when we got there it shot clear out of the water and just set there in the air looking at us while it et that fish it had caught, and it a foot long, and then it lit and wiggled down out of sight and then Pa—"

"What?" Jr. Pease said.

"—Pa he went in after it. It never taken him long to find it because he hadn't no more than got under until here they both come shooting out again and Pa on its back riding it"—he was hollering loud, now—"and then they went down again and the water boiled some, and then it got quiet and there wasn't nothing until after a while Pa come floating to the top and I—"

"What!" Jr. Pease said.

"—pulled him out and brung him home."

"Hurt bad?" Mr. Hayes asked.

"A goose-egg where it rammed his head into that holler log down there and sick some from swallering so much water, but mad more than anything else, so I reckon I better—"

"What in God's name was it?" Jr. Pease asked.

"A fish.—I better go get them shoes."

"What shoes!" Jr. Pease was hollering, too, now.

"Pa's, where he taken them off when he went in after it and I forgot to bring when I come on."

But we didn't have to decide right then, because it was a good hour before Ish got over his hurt enough to get away from Mrs. Theobold, so we had plenty of time to make up our minds whether a fish could get that big or not; and then it was quite a while before we could be proved right or wrong about it, because it was full dark when we left the creek bank and Ish still hadn't found it again.

It was not until about a month later. That boy came tearing down the road, pumping one of those mules in the sides with his heels. We could hear him hollering from the time he came into view, getting louder as he came on. He didn't even slow down, just slid that mule around in front of the store and headed back the way he had come (Mr. Hayes later claimed that mule didn't miss a beat), flinging us the words and dust and chips of dirt all together, "Pa says you all to come quick!"

So we went in a jog-trot down to the creek, all in a bunch, except Jr. Pease, who wouldn't wait on the rest of us and was way out in front of everybody. We found Ish squatted on the bank. The muddy water had dried and powdered him so that he looked like some old tree stump that had bleached and weathered out gray. He didn't turn as we came up or give any sign that he knew we were there.

After a while he spoke, but he might just have been thinking out loud, "There, now, he's done crawled up in that holler log."

"Crawled!" Jr. Pease said, maybe still confused about those shoes.

"Swum," Ish said, but you still couldn't be sure he had noticed us.

"How do you figure that?" Jr. Pease said. "I reckon you must got x-ray eyes if you can see through—"

But Ish was already easing down the bank into the water. And maybe he was still talking to himself when he said, "It'll take somebody to block up the other end of that log."

"You'll not get me in there with that thing," Jr. Pease said.

"Somebody tall," Ish said.

Nobody said anything, but we all looked at Big Jack. After a while, he gave a sheepish grin and began to take off his clothes. When he got his feet set at the end of the log, the water came just to his ears, so that he had to tilt his head back in order to clear his mouth and nose. Now and then he would cut his eyes our way and give that sheepish grin.

"I just can't bring myself to believe," Mr. Hayes said, "that a fish can get that big."

"I've claimed it all along," Jr. Pease said. "I was saying to somebody just the other day it was a sar-dine Ish—"

Maybe Ish was deaf. Anyway, he wasn't paying us any mind. He was easing out into deep water, and when he up-ended and went under, we might have missed it had not Jr. Pease stopped talking, because there wasn't a sound, hardly a ripple.

There was nothing to do but wait. We looked at Big Jack and he looked at us. He had that grin on his face again. We could hear a cow bawling in the Backburns' pasture half a mile away. Over at the Posers in the other direction, somebody was chopping wood. The corn in the field behind us whispered to the light breeze. Big Jack didn't make a sound either. Maybe he didn't have time. We nearly missed him, too, even though we were looking straight at him when it happened. One instant he was there, grinning at us; the next, he was gone, vanished.

"Et!" Jr. Pease whispered. "Swallered whole by—!"

But they both broke the surface at the same time. Big Jack wasn't hollering yet because he was choking on water.

"Why didn't you block him?" Ish said, admitting for the first time that any of us were there.

"Block, hell!" Big Jack hollered. "He's cut me to the bone as it is!"

It looked like it, when we pulled him up the bank, but soon the bleeding slowed, and then we could see they were not deep, just fin-cuts over each ankle. Ish hadn't come out. He was still diving.

Mr. Hayes got up from where he knelt by Big Jack and waited for Ish to surface again. "He's already gone back to where he come from, Ish. I reckon he understands we've only got one blacksmith to offer him."

Ish didn't answer because he was diving again.

The next day he and that boy blocked the end of that log with a piece of tin roofing, but they didn't find anything. "And won't, either," Mr. Hayes said. "I reckon it figures if it can whip the biggest of us and the maddest of us, why, what's left is not worth fooling with."

Maybe so. Anyway, we wore the subject out and quit talking about it, and most of us quit thinking about it, too. But not Ish. By sun-up, he would already have passed the store going down to that cornfield, and it would be full dark when he passed back on his way home, sitting in the wagon, frozen-faced, never speaking himself and only the barest nod when we spoke to him, and then not even that, as if like a downed tree in running water, he had at last petrified—a stone statue on that wagon seat and that boy beside him like a bigger one. So after a while we quit talking, and maybe we even quit noticing, except sometimes, before daylight, in that room in back of the store where I slept, hearing him pass I would wonder what he was thinking, hunched over on the seat of that empty wagon on his way to a field he must have laid by a month ago, so he had not even that for an excuse for spending the day on the creek bank staring at that muddy water.

So the summer passed and it got to be September, warm still, but the air beginning to take on the bright smell of fall. Everybody was harvesting, so Mr. Hayes and I were alone most of the day. It was early one morning. The sun was just beginning to take the chill off the air. Big Jack had left his shop, gone out to the Peases to look at their hay-baler that had quit on them. Mr. Hayes had his chair tilted back against the wall of the store porch and his eyes closed, though he wasn't asleep. I was busy, too, stirring the dust on the porch with a broom. So it was almost on us when we saw it—the wagon with just that boy on the seat, white-faced and stiff, with the lines held in one hand, letting the mules come on at their own slow pace, his other hand clamped to his side, and his clothes wet and muddy. Mr. Hayes went out and stopped the mules. "Where's Ish?" he asked, but the boy didn't respond, sitting wide-eyed and vacant as if in a trance, so Mr. Hayes asked again, and then we went around and looked into the wagon bed.

Ish looked back at us with all the spite and hate of a cornered rat. He was lying there, covered with feed sacks, glaring at us like some wild thing.

"What's the matter, Ish," Mr. Hayes asked, "are you hurt?" He reached over to pull away one of the sacks, but Ish screamed and snatched it back. Not quite in time, though. And I guess he must have known that we had seen, for the fire went out of him and he fell back and began to whimper. And then the mules moved on, either of their own will or maybe that boy had started them, and we watched them go on down the road, listening to the slow creak of the wagon as it turned into the yard, before we turned away and back to the store, Mr. Hayes being careful that our eyes did not meet. After a while, he said, "I reckon we never looked in that wagon. I reckon we never saw anything." I knew what he meant.

We got the story from the boy, but this was a long time afterwards, and it came like a picture puzzle to be pieced together, because he either could not or would not remember it.

It had come again. By whatever means he had of telling, Ish knew. And when it went into that blocked log, he knew that, too. So he had gone to meet it, leaving that boy on the bank to wait alone through the long, uneasy silence stretching on and on above the water motionless as a dirty windowpane until that parted scum, like man's last and ultimate sheet, met and covered it. Then the boy was diving, breaking scum and water and silence, to scrabble in the bottom mud for the log, touching and losing and finding it again and feeling in a wild flailing of arms for the opening. In time, his hands closed around Ish's ankles, just inside the mouth of the log. He pulled, but Ish didn't budge. He thrashed, kicked, jerked, but still couldn't free him. Ish was wedged. His lungs, throat were on fire. He braced his feet against the end of the log and in a final frenzied effort threw himself backwards. Ish came free, then; and something else, something that at first he heard rushing—roaring, he thought—at him, past him, and then came the bright shock of the breath-bursting blow in his side.

That was it. That was all he remembered, and even that much was in bits and pieces. The rest—how he managed to get himself and Ish into the wagon, why he had covered him, that Mr. Hayes had stopped the mules and we had looked at him—was gone. Or maybe it was never there to begin with.

So Mrs. Theobold was widowed, not four months later in the middle of winter when that boy pulled Ish out of the creek for the final time, but then, that day. Ish never left the house again but once—twice, if you count the time they carried him.

Not long after the funeral, Mrs. Theobold began looking

after Mr. Hayes and me, and once she told us about how Ish
would keep the shades drawn in that room he never left either.
"He said they kept laughing at him, the mules and the chickens and the hogs, raising their heads from the troughs and
laughing at him. At the last, even the trees and the grass in
the yard and the weeds in the road ditch got to where they kept
him awake at night. But he was a good man, Lord knows, he
was a good man."

There were six who carried him, but two could have done it
without strain. He was that little.

The Railroad
[1927]

The year Lindbergh flew the Atlantic alone, Mr. Hayes stole a railroad, not singlehanded, but with a little help from his friends and some of his men from the sawmill.

"Now, I suppose that train just followed you home," the sheriff said, when they finally found the locomotive and tender.

"Suppose anything you like," Mr. Hayes said. "It's on my property, and there it stays until I get what's owed me."

It didn't seem likely that the idea of the railroad would have originated with Mr. Billy Gusto, but it had. He came to the store one afternoon and asked Mr. Hayes, "What would you think of a railroad right here in Zions Cause?"

"For what?" Mr. Hayes asked.

"Why, to haul passengers from here to the Illinois Central line, where they could change and go wherever they want to."

"Not too many want to go anywhere."

"And no wonder. Now they have to get somebody to take them over there and come back and get them. With a regular connection service, there would be more. Besides, passengers

46

would just be a small part of it. Freight would be the big item. Crops going to markets that would pay more money than right around here. And then what about your sawmill? Now you're hauling lumber all the way to Princeton by wagon. You could just load it on a freight car right there at the sawmill and forget about it. Then along would come an engine and couple up to it and take it off and leave you an empty to fill when you got ready. Why, there could even be some track laid into the woods so you could bring the logs out to the mill. A railroad can't do anything but help your business, and it will put Zions Cause on the map. It's all that's needed for this place to grow."

"And who would build it?" Mr. Hayes asked.

"I would and will if I can line up enough business to get started," Mr. Billy said. "You think about it. I'll talk to you again in a few days."

Mr. Billy, they said, was born with a silver spoon in his mouth. His father, who had been a native of the next county, had land and money, too, and Mr. Billy was the only child. He grew up without drive or much interest in anything except indolence. When he was eighteen, the old man, in an effort to give him some polish, enrolled him in a college in Virginia, only to learn too late to do anything about it that Mr. Billy had dropped out after attending the first day. He had spent his time instead in the company of a local girl he had met. When they had married—some say just one jump ahead of the stork—and come home and told him, the story is that the old man spent the entire day locked up in the barn with a jug of whiskey and a pistol, blowing bottles and whatever else he could find to smithereens. When he finished the jug, he blew that to smithereens, too, and came out and gave them three hundred acres in what was to become Zions Cause and built a fine house on it for them to live in. The land was farmed, when Mr. Billy could get somebody to do it for him. His time was spent fathering daughters, seven of them before he quit, and playing the role of what he considered to be a country gentleman and tapping the old man for money to keep them going. In what must have been sheer desperation, the old man, before he died, converted most of his holdings into cash, knowing that Mr. Billy would soon piecemeal it all away, anyhow, and tied it up in a trust. Upon his death, a sizable sum came to Mr. Billy and the first thing he did was go out and buy a Pierce Arrow touring car to haul Mrs. Gusto and those girls around in. Mr. Billy's whole life had been dedicated to ease and self-indulgence so it was uncharacteristic of him even to conceive of the idea, much less become fired up about it.

Mr. Hayes could see merit in the idea and benefit not only for his own enterprises but also for Zions Cause, whose welfare he considered his business, too. So when Mr. Billy came back, he told him to count on his support.

"I wonder if that support would run to an advance," Mr. Billy said.

"What do you mean?"

"Well, say you make me an advance on services to be rendered and say I give you a note saying the company will either provide the service or pay back the advance with interest at the going rate. And knowing that I'll have your business, I'll go ahead and lay a spur line out to your sawmill and it won't cost you a dime."

"What size advance have you got in mind?"

"I was thinking about fifteen thousand," Mr. Billy said. "It would keep me from having to sell something I want to hang on to."

"Sounds to me like you're thinking about a partner, not an advance," Mr. Hayes said. "What's the total cost of this thing going to run, anyway?"

Mr. Billy told him. Mr. Hayes whistled.

"Now, that includes the rolling stock, all reconditioned and in good shape," Mr. Billy said. "The Illinois Central is going to carry me on that."

That an outfit like the Illinois Central would think enough of the enterprise to furnish equipment on time was enough to sway Mr. Hayes, but Mr. Billy went even further. "I'll even extend your spur line on into the woods so you can haul the logs back to your mill, and all it will cost you will be the use of the engine. In the long run, I ought to come out on it, at least break even. Now, what do you say?"

"Draw up the papers," Mr. Hayes told him.

So the Zions Cause Railroad Company was formed with Mr. Billy as sole owner and president, and the railroad was built. It ran three and two-tenths miles from a little station just a hundred yards south of the store to another just like it where it connected with the Illinois Central main line, with a spur running off to the sawmill.

The day the train made its first run was an occasion for celebration. Although it was not scheduled to get into Zions Cause until the middle of the afternoon—it was coming all the way from the factory in Chicago—by ten o'clock in the morning the first wagons began pulling into the field beside the station. By noon, you took your life in your hands if you stepped out into the road in front of the store. If a wagon or a Model T Ford didn't get you, you could count on being run into and knocked down and trampled under by that mob of young ones ripping and romping up and down between the store and the station. Mrs. Theobold gave me my orders in no uncertain terms, while Mr. Hayes looked on and grinned in both approval of her and sympathy for me.

Jr. Pease came into the store with a half-dollar and bought some red ribbon and asked for his change in pennies.

"Now what are you up to?" Mr. Hayes asked.

"I'm going to lay them on the track and let that train mash them flat," he said. "Then I'm going to take them over to Big Jack's blacksmith shop and put a hole in them and put some of this here ribbon through them and sell them for souvenirs."

"What are you going to ask for them?"

"I reckon I can get a dime out of each one."

"I'll just bet you can, too," Mr. Hayes told him, and then he turned to me. "Remind me to lock up the next time you see him headed in this direction. Anybody that can sell a flat penny for a dime, well, I'm just not smart enough to do business with."

When we had finished lunch, Mr. Hayes finally took pity on me. "Now, I'm not countermanding Mrs. Theobold's orders, but I've got a job for you to do. I want you to go down to the station and buy us two round-trip tickets before they all get sold. And then stay there and watch for that train, and when it gets here, you come and get me. And don't forget you're working."

The station platform was already almost full, and in that field on the other side of the tracks, they were packing up the leftovers of their basket dinners and putting them away in the cars and wagons and drifting over to line that side. I bought the tickets and moved on up the track to get away from their noise so I could hear the train far enough away to have time to run and get Mr. Hayes before it got there. I saw Jr. Pease up there by himself and joined him. He had his pennies all laid out on the track and was standing guard over them.

"I wish they would come on," he said. "I need to get started if I'm going to put holes in these things and ribbons through them before they get back."

"You're not going?" I asked.

"Naw. I must of run that track from one end to the other at least a dozen times already. Why pay to see what I've already seen for nothing?"

Then we heard it, first the whistle, then the chugging, but it was slowing down and finally stopped.

"What's the matter?" I asked.

"They're switching into the sawmill spur to turn around," he said. "They'll come backing into the station so they'll be headed right to go out."

I didn't know how he knew so much about it, but it made sense to me.

Suddenly, I remembered Mr. Hayes and went tearing off to the store. I yelled at him through the door and got back to Jr. Pease just about the time the train got through backing and filling. There were two long blasts on the whistle, and then the chugging started hard, getting faster as it came on.

Then we could see it, the rear end of the passenger coach all decked out in red, white and blue bunting with an American flag sticking up on each side; and behind it, the coal tender and then the engine, rolling out black smoke and a white cloud of steam hissing out between the wheels; and Mr. Billy hanging out the window of the cab and the engineer trying to see around him. Then Mr. Billy disappeared and that whistle cut loose again. The crowd gave a cheer, and I was yelling, too, and jumping up and down and managed to step on Mr. Hayes, who had come to stand beside me. Then the whistle stopped, and Mr. Billy popped his head out the window again, shoving the engineer aside and blocking his view, waving his arms and grinning.

I guess that engineer finally decided he had run that engine long enough blind, because he threw on the brakes and locked the driving wheels. But the train kept on coming, hissing and screeching against the rails, and throwing out a shower of sparks from the wheels as they passed us. The passenger coach and the tender rolled over Jr. Pease's pennies, but the engine drivers sliding along knocked them in all directions. Jr. Pease was onto the track looking for them almost before that engine could get out of his way.

Along about then, it began to dawn on them on the station platform and the ones on the other side of the tracks and on us, too, what that engineer must have been reasonably sure of for some time, that the train wasn't going to be able to stop, and so they began to try to clear the platform and put some distance between them and the tracks. They managed somehow to get back out of the way without any of them getting seriously trampled before the rear end of the passenger coach made kindling wood out of that barricade that had been built there to stop it. But in the process of being demolished that barricade did what it was meant to do. The train stopped with a good two feet to spare before it ran out of track.

Mr. Hayes and I had been tearing along the side of the

tracks chasing the engine, and when it stopped we caught up and passed it and so were the first on the scene to inspect the damage. It wasn't all that much, just the guardrail around the platform of the passenger coach bent and the door glass shattered, but when they rebuilt that barricade they were going to have to start from scratch.

Mr. Billy and the engineer jumped down out of the engine cab and came running back to see how bad it was. When he had satisfied himself that there was no serious damage, Mr. Billy said, "You are sure not much of an engineer."

"Neither are you," the engineer told him.

"Well, I don't pretend to be."

"Then stay out of the cab and let me do my job," the engineer said and started back to the engine.

"It's my railroad and I ride any damn where I please!" Mr. Billy hollered after him. But we noticed he didn't follow. Instead, he went in to join Mrs. Gusto and those girls in the front of the passenger coach.

The coach had been oversold. By the time Mr. Hayes and I got in, there wasn't a seat to be had and the aisle was full, but it worked out all right because we found a place outside on the rear platform and that was better than being inside. As we pulled out of the station, we passed Jr. Pease standing beside the track. He reached out and caught a handhold and swung aboard as if it were something he did every day of his life.

"How did the pennies come out?" Mr. Hayes asked him.

"Too flat to spend and not flat enough to sell," he said. "They needed that engine."

I said, "I thought you told me you weren't coming, that you wouldn't pay to see what you had already seen for nothing."

"I wouldn't," he said. "Anyway, this fool thing has done

ruined enough of my pennies to pay for a ticket and has run me out of business to boot."

In spite of the minor misadventure, the railroad was well begun and soon appeared to be flourishing. While the passenger coach didn't run full on its two trips a day, it didn't run empty either. The railroad opened up the outside world to the people of Zions Cause. It got to be the thing for a while for whole families to go to Princeton or Dawson Springs or in the other directon to Paducah for the day, taking the Zions Cause line to the far station and then changing to the Illinois Central for other points. Some ventured even farther. Jr. Pease was once gone for a week and then came back and claimed he had been all the way to Chicago, dodging conductors and porters the whole time, still trying, I guess, to get even over those pennies.

For a time, on Sunday afternoons, Mr. Billy would load Mrs. Gusto and those girls and anybody else who wanted to go into that passenger coach and run the train up and down the line, giving that whistle a good workout and maybe stopping somewhere for a picnic. He had got another engineer who was local to the area, if not to Zions Cause itself, and who would tolerate him in the cab of the engine. And there were always enough volunteer firemen. But after a month or two, Mr. Billy's interest flagged, and the excursions became less and less frequent and finally stopped altogether.

From the first, the freight business had been especially good, particularly the output from the sawmill. Mr. Hayes was soon shipping all the lumber he could produce and staying up half the night trying to keep up with his business correspondence and to find a place for the money that came pouring in.

Oh, Mr. Hayes knew what to do with the money—what he had done with any spare cash he had—buy land with it. In the years since he had started the store, and later the sawmill, he had slowly accumulated a number of parcels and farms. Now that the lumber business was booming, his empire was beginning to expand at a considerable rate. And he recognized that a good part of it was owing to the railroad and Mr. Billy.

So when Mr. Billy failed to follow through on his promise to extend the sawmill spur into the woods, Mr. Hayes was hesitant about mentioning it to him, delayed doing so, in fact, for several months. But finally, when production began to suffer noticeably because they were now having to haul the logs so far to the sawmill, Mr. Hayes went to see him about it.

"I know I said I'd do it," Mr. Billy told him, "but right now I've got a money problem."

"That's hard to understand," Mr. Hayes said. "Surely the railroad is showing a profit."

"Oh, it's showing a profit, all right. It's just not making any money."

"I seem a little slow," Mr. Hayes said. "You may have to explain that to me."

"Well, it's simple enough. That advance of yours was spent before I even got the thing running, so it's like I'm hauling for you for free. And the other business don't hardly bring in enough to pay operating expenses, so I'm having to sink more and more of my own money into it. And then there's the payments to the Illinois Central for the equipment; there's not much way that I can keep them up."

"But surely," Mr. Hayes said, "you must have foreseen this would happen and set aside a reserve to take care of it."

"Well, what I didn't foresee, and what nobody ever bothered to tell me and I had to wait this long to find out, was that a big part of the money my daddy left me, he tied up where I can't touch the principal. And now I've done spent down to where I've not got a free dime except the interest, and I need that to live on."

"You've got your land. You could raise some on that."

"No sir! I'm not touching that land. It's all I've got left for sure, that and the interest. Besides, that blamed railroad is not worth it. It has been nothing but worry and grief to me ever since I started it. I'm at the point now where I just want to be shut of it and forget it."

"You mean sell it?" Mr. Hayes asked.

"Not exactly."

"What, then?"

"The deal I made with the Illinois Central was that they would furnish the equipment with a little something down and I would pay it out on a regular schedule; and if I didn't, the line would be theirs."

"And you agreed to that?"

"It seemed all right at the time."

"Then ask for an extension," Mr. Hayes said. "Surely they will give you a little time."

"They've already given me an extension. Two, in fact, but that's as far as they'll go. If I don't cover the back payments by the end of the month—and I wouldn't, even if I had the money to do it with—they take over the whole line."

"How much?" Mr. Hayes asked.

Mr. Billy picked up a letter on his desk. "Eight thousand

seven hundred and sixty-two dollars and thirty-nine cents, including penalties," he said.

"Just what do you plan to do about my advance? There's still around nine thousand that hasn't been used up in services yet."

"That's not my concern," Mr. Billy said. "You made that deal with the Zions Cause Railroad Company and come the end of the month the company is going to belong to the Illinois Central."

Mr. Hayes didn't bother to argue with him about it. He had known Mr. Billy for a good part of both their lives and in spite of that had trusted him in a business deal, so he couldn't really blame Mr. Billy. He came straight home and wrote the president of the Illinois Central, asking if he would honor the obligation outstanding on the advance. Ten days later he received a reply from the legal division saying no.

Mr. Hayes then took the train to Paducah and spent some time talking with a lawyer and came back discouraged.

"Chances are less than fifty-fifty that I could win," he said, "but win or lose, I'd say it's an absolute certainty that the legal fees would run more than the amount."

The next day he spent in his chair on the store porch, staring off into space.

And the next three days he spent walking that railroad track from end to end, and cornering that locomotive engineer and asking a thousand questions, and strolling up and down the logging road that ran from the sawmill into the woods where they were cutting, with his head down studying the ground.

Then he made up his mind.

"Possession," he said, "is nine-tenths of the law. If it was on my property, it would give me that advantage. And then, too, they'd have to come to me, and that helps."

The last day of the month, Mr. Hayes stole the entire Zions Cause Railroad. Well, not really all of it. What track was in sight of either station, he left, but he took all the rest.

He used the hands from the sawmill. And that engineer was in on it, paid at the rate, he claimed, of three thousand dollars a month but admitted that Mr. Hayes only used him for a day and a half. And word got around of what Mr. Hayes was doing and why, so there were a number of volunteers. Jr. Pease was one who insisted on having a part in it and worked like a dog the whole time, obviously enjoying every minute of it. Tearing up a railroad must have been sweet revenge to him.

They pulled up the spikes and loaded them and the rails and the crossties on the freight cars as they came along. When the cars were filled, they ran down to the sawmill spur, which was on Mr. Hayes' land, and stacked them neatly on the side. The last load they left on the cars and left them standing on the spur. Then they took out a couple of sections of rail from behind the engine and tender and moved them in front and ran forward on them. Repeating that process, they walked that engine and tender all the way to the end of the logging road and hid it with brush. And then they went home and waited.

They didn't have to wait too long. Two days later, the Illinois Central dropped a two-man crew and a handcar off at the junction with orders to bring all the equipment to that end. They rounded that first bend after leaving the station and ran that handcar onto the roadbed, still pumping, I guess, before they noticed that the rails had quit. They walked on down the roadbed a mile or so looking for them and then gave up and went back and got that handcar back on the rails and went back to the station and waited. Jr. Pease, who was hiding and watching, said they had to sit there the whole day before a work train came along and picked them up.

The next day, we had a railroad detective in on us. He seemed like a decent enough man, and I felt sorry for him because there was no way he was going to be able to do his job without looking like a fool. He had to wet his lips a time or two before he could get it out.

"Anybody see what happened to that railroad?"

Jr. Pease, sitting on the edge of the store porch with the rest of them behind him listening, said seriously, "Not me. I been setting here whittling on this stick all morning and I ain't hardly had time to look up. I must have missed it."

The detective turned red. He opened his mouth once or twice, but nothing came out. Finally, he turned and walked off in the direction of the station.

He walked the length of that roadbed and back that day and all the way to the brushpile at the end of that logging road but didn't find anything except what was obvious to everyone: the stack of rails and crossties and pile of spikes and those freight cars and the passenger coach on the sawmill spur.

The next day he had the sheriff with him and two deputies. They found it, but wouldn't have if they had had any sense. One of those deputies was out there roaming through that thick woods looking for it. I know that's hard to believe, but that's what he was doing. He happened to come up on the back side of that brush pile, and of course there it was.

The sheriff and that railroad detective came to the store to see what Mr. Hayes had to say about it.

"You go back and tell your people," Mr. Hayes told the detective, "that my position is this: regardless of how it got there, it's on my property, and there it'll stay until I get what's owed me."

A week later a car pulled up in front of the store with two men in it. They got out and came in asking for Mr. Hayes. The one who did the talking turned out to be the lawyer from the Illinois Central who had answered Mr. Hayes' letter.

Since there was no one but us, Mr. Hayes took them to the back of the store where he had his desk and dealt with them there. The second man found a seat on an empty nail keg, but the lawyer preferred to stand. He didn't bother with any preliminaries.

"About our railroad you stole," he said.

"You are jumping to two conclusions," Mr. Hayes said. "First, that it is in fact your railroad, and second, that I stole it. Neither one of these things has been established."

"We want it back."

"As soon as I get my money."

"We will initiate criminal proceedings against you."

"Go right ahead. It's my home county and the judge will know who I am."

"Civil action, too."

"Same thing holds, plus you're a big, rich outfit from out of state trying to beat a little local man out of a sizable chunk of his hard-earned money. Besides, if you're any good at your job, you'll know you don't have a hundred percent sure case."

"We'll appeal until we get a judgment in our favor."

"And it will wind up costing you more than what you'll be saving, not to mention what the newspapers are going to do to your public image when they run their David and Goliath stories."

The second man had been sitting listening. He said quietly, "Herman."

The lawyer turned and looked at him.

"Go out and get yourself some fresh air. It'll do you good. Walk down and look over that little station. I'll be along in a few minutes."

The lawyer stared at him for a minute, then clamped his mouth shut tight and wheeled around and left, banging the screen door after him.

When he had gone, the man said, "I'm John Robbins. I'm the one you wrote your letter to, but it didn't get all the way up to me. Now, I'm not saying the answer would have been any different if it had. Herman is one of the best, and I don't often go against him."

He paused then and looked around the store. I had been leaning against the wall, listening. He smiled and winked at me.

"Is this your boy?" he asked Mr. Hayes.

"No, that's my partner," Mr. Hayes told him. He introduced me, and Mr. Robbins got up and shook hands and said he was glad to meet me, sounding as if he meant it.

"Well, now," he said to me, "if you're anything like he is, I can see I'm going to have my hands full."

Mr. Hayes said, "We kind of learn from each other."

"You're fortunate," Mr. Robbins said. He shifted on the nail keg so he could talk to both of us. "Gentlemen, we've got a problem. Maybe it will wind up in court, but we don't know that yet. I'd like to see us explore some other alternatives."

He waited, and when Mr. Hayes didn't say anything, he went on.

"We seem to have got started out on the wrong foot. That happens sometimes, and when it does, the best thing is to try to start over. I came all the way down here from Chicago, quite frankly because I wanted to meet a man who would go as far as to steal a whole railroad. And if 'steal' bothers you, I'll be glad to change it to 'seize' or 'confiscate' or whatever suits you. I came down here in a private Pullman car, a little added something that goes with my job. It's sitting on a siding in Princeton. My wife came with me. I work a lot, and it gives us a chance to be together. I know she would enjoy meeting both of you. What I am getting at is this: why don't you join us for dinner—or supper or whatever the right name for it is. That will give us a chance to get acquainted. Then afterwards, the four of us will see if we can work anything out."

He smiled at Mr. Hayes. "You see, she's my partner."

"What time?" Mr. Hayes asked.

"About eight."

But then he read my expression.

"No, make it seven," he said.

That was still going to be an hour and a half past our suppertime.

Mrs. Theobold took a lot of pains with me. And Mr. Hayes took a lot of pains with himself. At last, we both passed muster, and we got in the car and started for Princeton. Mr. Hayes slowed down the last half of the way, but we still got there half an hour early.

That private Pullman would have made two or three of the passenger coach on the Zions Cause line. Mr. Robbins met us at the door and ushered us in. It was the finest room I had ever seen, richly carpeted and draped, with one part furnished as a sitting room and the other as a dining room. And somewhere back of that paneled partition, there must have been a kitchen and a bedroom.

Mrs. Robbins was sitting on the couch when we came in. She stood up to meet us. She was a little younger than her husband. She must have been in her late thirties or early forties. Her hair was soft brown and cut short and fit her head like a cap. Her smile was wide and warm and made her eyes crinkle as she put out her hand to Mr. Hayes.

"I've been wondering how you would look," she said. "I've never met anyone before who has made off with an entire railroad."

Then she turned to me.

"I've been wondering about you, too, but I haven't had much time. I just found out about you this morning."

"Please sit down," she said to Mr. Hayes, indicating a chair. "And you," she said to me, "you come sit with me on the couch."

As we were settling ourselves, a black man in a white coat came through the door at the other end of the room. "Here is William for the drink orders," she said to me. "Why don't you and I have some orange juice. Mr. Hayes may want something stronger, and I know John will."

So we sat and sipped and talked. I noticed that Mr. Robbins, and soon Mr. Hayes, too, didn't talk to her as a woman but as a person, an equal, not only seeking her opinions but considering them. And none of them talked down to me. I felt natural and at ease. After a while, the black man, William, came in to see if we wanted refills and to say that the meal was almost ready.

"William takes good care of us," she told me. "I'm afraid he even spoils us."

"Mrs. Theobold takes care of us," I said.

She looked at me then, and I knew what she wanted to ask but wouldn't, so I told her.

"She died when I was born. My father had already disappeared. Do you have any children?"

Her smile faded, and the look of sadness which replaced it told me I had touched a tender spot. I wanted to change the subject but couldn't think of anything. Mr. Hayes and her husband had been listening. I guess they couldn't think of anything either. She got us out of it. She took my hand and squeezed it and then said, "You must be starved. I'll bet it's way past your mealtime."

"I could eat," I said.

As if on cue, William came in and told us it was ready. We went to the table, and I held her chair and surprised Mr. Hayes. When we were seated, William brought us each a small bowl of clear soup. I reached for my spoon and then realized I was in trouble. There were too many of them, too many in fact of everything, and I had not the faintest notion of what to use first. I looked across the table at Mr. Hayes, but he was staring at all that silverware with a bewildered look on his face. Then I felt her foot gently touch mine. I looked at her, and without looking at me or interrupting what she was saying, she reached out and picked up one of her spoons. I found the one of mine that matched, and Mr. Hayes, who was watching, found his. So the meal went on, dish after dish, without embarrassment.

Though I had no idea of half of what I ate, it was all good, maybe because I was so hungry. The conversation was easy and interesting. They wanted to know about Mr. Hayes and me, and they told us about themselves. They had been born into wealth, both of them. Even so, you don't come to run a railroad as large as the Illinois Central without struggle. They spoke of their hard times as if they were the best times of their lives.

When the meal was over, we all complimented William and moved back to the sitting area. William brought drinks in tiny glasses. What was in the glasses was deep red and looked delicious. Mrs. Robbins saw me eyeing them and lifted an eyebrow to Mr. Hayes.

"Ask him," Mr. Hayes told her.

I nodded, and she told William to bring one for me. It was not as good as it looked, but it wasn't bad either.

After we had finished and William had cleared away, she moved closer to me so that we were touching and found my hand. It gave me a warm, cozy feeling, and I could have sat there all night.

"Now tell us about this claim of yours," Mr. Robbins said, getting down to what we were there for.

Mr. Hayes told them.

"Herman was probably right," he said. "We could win."

"Maybe," Mr. Hayes said. "But at great expense in money and reputation."

"He's right, you know, John," she said. "I can just picture what the papers would do with that story."

"Of course he's right," Mr. Robbins said. "Well, it looks as if we've got each other over a barrel. Your claim is a little shaky, but if we go to court, we lose even if we win. How do we negotiate our way out of this? What is your proposal?"

"What will you do with the railroad if you get it back?" Mr. Hayes asked.

"I don't know. Get the equipment out of there for sure. Maybe leave the rest."

"The repayment of the advance with interest was only a secondary condition of my agreement. The first condition, and the one I'm the most interested in, was for freight service. I need that for my business."

"How much shipping have you done in, say, the last six months?"

Mr. Hayes told him. He rested his chin on his fingertips and stared at the ceiling for a while.

"What if we agreed to run down to your mill on a regular basis and pick up your freight at the same rate you're paying now?"

"Then I would be satisfied," Mr. Hayes told him.

"Well, I wouldn't," Mr. Robbins said. "There is still the matter of three miles of track to be relaid, not to mention getting that engine out of the woods."

"How did you ever get to be such a horsetrader?" Mr. Hayes asked.

He laughed and she joined him. "How do you think I got to be president of the Illinois Central?"

They talked on, settling the details. My eyes had been getting heavy for some time. Finally, they closed.

I awoke in her arms, my head on her breast. It was late, and we were leaving. They came to the car with us, she with her arm around me, guiding because I was having a hard time walking straight. She put me in the car and said, "How about a hug?"

I gave her one and a kiss, too.

Mr. Robbins leaned in from the other side and patted me on the shoulder. Then he shook hands with Mr. Hayes.

"I don't know whether we will ever see each other again," he said, "but I want you to know, tonight has been one of the most enjoyable times of our lives."

"Ours, too," Mr. Hayes said.

As we drove away, we both looked back. They were standing with their arms around each other, watching us off.

I turned around, still feeling warm and cozy, and looked at Mr. Hayes. He smiled and patted my knee, but it was a sad smile. I knew that we were both thinking of Susan, my mother, but in different ways. It was my last thought before sleep overtook me again.

The Baptism of
Lucinda Blackburn
[1930]

Although there were several to choose from in Zions Cause,
Amos Blackburn went all the way to Paducah to find him a wife.
Soon after he returned, he brought her down to Mr. Hayes'
store to show her off. Her name was Lucinda, and she was
right much of a woman, tall, taller by a head than Amos, and
big-boned, but rather pretty in the face. Mr. Hayes remarked
later that she looked like she might just bust out fat any minute. He was wrong about that. It was more like three months.
Some were satisfied that she was In The Family Way; others
doubted that a man no bigger than Amos could actually im-
pregnate a woman that size. It was the subject of some contro-
versy for a while. As it turned out, she was not In The Family
Way, just fat—well, fleshy, if you wanted to be polite about
it—which didn't conclusively prove, as the doubters claimed,
that Amos couldn't, only that he hadn't.

In the succeeding months Lucinda grew even fleshier. She
surpassed her mother-in-law, old Mrs. Blackburn, who could

tip the scales at two hundred without strain, and just kept going.

"It must be the result," Mr. Hayes speculated, "of holding herself in all that time. Now that she's married and feels safe to relax, this is the repercussion."

Whether Mr. Hayes was right about it or not, Lucinda went on to become, indisputably, the biggest woman in Zions Cause.

Now, the significance of that lay not entirely in the honor that accompanies such a superlative, though it is not my intent to belittle that. As Mr. Hayes was wont to remark, everybody ought to be tops in something, even if it's just producing the most ear wax, say, or having the smelliest feet. It sets a person apart, gives him substance and individuality, not to mention provides his neighbors with a standard of excellence, a goal to strive for, or against, as the case may be. In those days I wasn't always able to tell whether Mr. Hayes was serious or not. Several years had to pass before I would come to the realization that no one speaks entirely in jest.

No, the significance was related to the fact that Lucinda, coming as she did from Paducah, where people were maybe not as careful about some things as they might have been, had not been scripturally baptized. Oh, Lucinda *thought* she had fulfilled the requirements. It took Brother Bois Carmichael, who was then pastor of Zions Cause Church, to set her straight.

Brother Bois was strong on Doctrine. "Baptism," he declared, "means total immersion. When the Lord was baptized of John in Jordan in Mark 1 and 4, it says He came straightway up out of the water. Now, to come up out of the water, He first had to be in it. He had to be *under* it, if you please. Immersed! It ain't no other way. And the Scripture clearifies that in Ephesians 4 and 5 when it says one Lord, one faith, *one baptism!*" Brother Bois could chop logic with the best of them.

Although you couldn't call Brother Bois a preacherboy—he must have been at least forty-five—he was new to the ministry. In fact, Zions Cause was his first pastorate. Brother Bois had come to the Lord later in life than most. The ministry was his second career. In his first, he was fifteen years keeping the accounts of a large building supply company in Paducah.

Brother Bois was particular—you might say, and some did, even finicky—and not only about doctrine. He wanted, needed, even felt a compulsion to see things done just so. "If you can't do it right," Brother Bois would say, "then you got no business messing with it a-tall." Maybe it came from having been so long a bookkeeper, an occupation which forces the mind to focus on and value details, demands persistent precision and bottom-line accuracy.

Brother Bois was unmarried, at least as far as anybody knew. "Made of hisself an eunuch for the Kingdom of Heaven's sake," was one theory. "Born a old maid," was another. "Stick of a man like that, who'd have him?" Mrs. Blackburn was rumored to have said in confidence to somebody. "Why, poke you to death to sleep in the bed with him." Whether she said it or not, there was no denying: Brother Bois was skinny in the extreme.

The matter of Lucinda's deficiency became public the Sunday she, on Mrs. Blackburn's orders, no doubt, presented herself for membership in Zions Cause Church. By Letter. Mr. Hayes explained that to me later, though how he knew was beyond me, since he wasn't a member himself and never attended.

"There are two ways," he told me. "One is on a Profession of Faith and as a Candidate for Baptism. That's the one you use if you're starting out from scratch. The other is by presenting a letter of endorsement from a church you already belong to. Course, it has to be the same kind of church, and in Lucinda's case, there's the rub. It seems that church she belonged to in Paducah sprinkled their members rather than soused them."

"This is not just a simple case of Foreign Baptism," Brother Bois told the congregation, standing there at the front of the church, waving the Letter, with Lucinda there beside him, tall as he was and a good three times as thick, head bowed, hands clasped in front of her. "I'm afraid, Beloved, it's a case of no baptism a-tall!"

(Mr. Hayes explained that to me, too. Foreign Baptism is where the sending church differs in some insignificant particular from the receiving church. In such a case, the receiving church may elect to overlook the discrepancy and accept the applicant anyway. But, now, if the difference involves something as serious as baptism, why, then, the receiving church has no discretion in the matter.)

"My recommendation to you," Brother Bois said after some consideration, "is we deny membership to this applicant on the strength of her Letter, but extend it to her with welcome arms on her Profession of Faith and the presentation of herself as a Candidate for Baptism."

Old Mrs. Blackburn was mortified. She hissed across Rile,

her oldest son in whom she was well pleased, and his wife and offspring to Amos, her next in whom at the moment, at least, she was not, at the far end of her pew: "You said she was a Christian!"

"She is!" Amos hissed back.

"Not until she's been baptized," Brother Bois said. He had been following the exchange along with the rest of us. "Not entirely, she ain't."

"Well, do it then!" Amos said.

"You can't decide for her. She'll have to ask it herself. And then the church will have to vote on it."

"Does that mean you're going to stick my head under the water?" Lucinda asked.

"Baptism means total immersion."

"Oh, Lordy!"

"Aw come on, now, Lucinder," Amos said, "it ain't going to kill you."

"Looks to me like it's the least she could do," Mrs. Blackburn snorted. Before Lucinda, Mrs. Blackburn had been the biggest woman in Zions Cause. Still was, in everything but size. Born to the purple, according to Mr. Hayes, and accustomed to command.

"I just can't help it," Lucinda said. "I'm skeered to death of water."

At ten years old, I was somewhat surprised that anyone of that size would have been scared of anything and said as much to Mr. Hayes later when I was filling him in on what had gone on.

"You must learn not to depend too much on outward appearances," he said. "They say elephants are scared of mice, though I don't know that for a fact. Did Lucinda finally agree to be immersed?"

"Yes, but it seems to me such a picky thing for them to insist on. And I'm sure nobody would have if Brother Bois hadn't stuck his horn in."

"Well, logically, I expect he was right. But practically, though he may not have realized it yet, I believe he's just been hoist with his own petard."

I didn't understand, and Mr. Hayes didn't always explain. He held to the belief that it was a vital part of my education to find some things out for myself.

"Somehow that sounds smutty," I said. "Is it something I can say around Mrs. Theobold?" Mrs. Theobold was the lady who took care of Mr. Hayes and me, and she had high standards which she didn't hesitate to impose on me.

"Better not. It's a perfectly respectable expression, but if it sounds off-color to you, it'll sound even more so to her."

It was good advice. The meaning, when I finally worked it out, was, as Mr. Hayes had said, perfectly respectable, but the derivation would have, beyond doubt, got my mouth washed out with soap.

I don't know just when Brother Bois came to the realization that he may have been hoisted. Some time before anybody else, except Mr. Hayes, of course. Our first clue was when he came to the store early one morning to borrow an axe and saw.

"Taking down a tree in the front yard," he told Mr. Hayes. "It's growing crooked."

"If you're talking about that old oak, it's been growing that way for twenty years at least. It was there when they built the parsonage. They decided to leave it for shade."

"Too old to try to straighten up now. Only thing to do is take it out."

I fetched him our axe and bucksaw. Still he lingered. Finally, he asked, "How much do you reckon that thing weighs, say, by the foot?"

"No idea," Mr. Hayes said. "Why do you ask?"

"Just curious," he said and left.

"Does he have the right to do that?" I asked Mr. Hayes. "After all, the parsonage belongs to the church, not him." Actually, the land that both the parsonage and the church stood on had originally belonged to Mr. Hayes. He had donated it as well as some of the material for the buildings to the congregation.

"It's debatable, but that's not the question. I wonder why he would want to do it in the first place."

"Why, he just told us. It's crooked. And you know how he is about everything being just so."

"I know that's what he said."

"Well, why else, then?"

"Ah," Mr. Hayes said. "That's the question."

Since we had no answer, we had to leave it hanging. In the next few days the old oak was cut down, sawed up and cleared away and our tools returned—sharper and shinier than when they left.

Lucinda's baptismal service had been set for a week from the following Sunday at two in the afternoon at the usual place, that spot on the piece of land Mr. Hayes had bought from Mrs. Theobold after her husband died where the creek made a bend and formed a good-sized pool. As the day approached, talk at the store began to touch on the event, and, inevitably, the problem emerged.

"How in the Holy Hell," somebody finally wondered, "is a beanpole like Brother Bois ever going to handle a woman like Lucinder Blackburn?"

There it was—the significance. I looked at Mr. Hayes. He was studying his fingernails. If he was thinking about petards, he didn't say so.

"If he did manage somehow to get her under," somebody else said, "why, it ain't no way he'd ever be able to raise her up again."

"Especially, not with her fighting him ever step of the way."

"Aw, she better not try that. Old Mrs. Blackburn would tear the skin right off her backside with her tongue."

Herman Poser, who was timid and always sat in the background and never volunteered anything, forgot himself and spoke. "Fat folks float," he said softly.

We all looked at him in surprise.

"Herman's right!" somebody said. "They do. And the fatter they are the harder they float. So it'll be not only her weight and resistance he'll have to deal with when he tries to dunk her. Is that what you had in mind, Herman?"

Herman grinned and nodded and, wonder of wonders, spoke again. "And skinny folks," he said with some confidence, "they sink."

Everybody agreed, but nobody saw any significance in it, so Herman faded into the background again.

"If I was him," somebody said, "I'd find me a elephant or something to practice on, I wouldn't just try it cold."

"Of course!" Mr. Hayes said and hit himself on the forehead with the heel of his hand.

"Of course what?" they wanted to know.

"Oh, nothing," Mr. Hayes said and grinned to himself.

"Of course what?" I asked as soon as we were alone.

"Of course he wouldn't just try it cold. He'd find him something to practice on."

"Like an elephant?"

"No. More like maybe an oak log."

I couldn't believe it. I had to see it myself. The next morning early without saying anything to anybody I struck out through the woods, circled around and found me a good spot in that locust thicket that borders the back of the parsonage, and sure enough, there it was—a section of that old tree he had taken down about six feet long with the stumps of two limbs sticking out like arms, ready for him in the middle of the yard. I didn't have long to wait. Right away he came out and threw out the dishwater from his breakfast dishes, and in a few minutes here he came out again ready for business— black suit pants, white shirt, tie and everything.

He had some trouble getting that log up on its end, but he finally managed it, and stood there bracing it with his shoulder and resting himself a bit. He took some time getting his feet placed just right and when he had them set to suit him, drew in a deep breath, closed his eyes and raised his right hand. "Lucinda Blackburn," he intoned, "I baptize thee in the name of the Father and the Son and the Holy Ghost."

He brought his hand down and placed it on the log about where the back of her neck would be, with his other hand covered her mouth and nose and tilted the log back until it was slanting at about a forty-five-degree angle to the ground. He held it there for a moment then tried to raise it up again. I could see the cords in his neck standing out, mouth twisting to one side, arms quivering with the strain, and I could hear him grunting. Finally, he had to shift his feet, move his hands and get his shoulder under it. "A-men," he said when it was erect again, but there was no triumph in it. He was way short of the mark.

"Thought I'd find you here," Mr. Hayes said and caused me to scratch my arm on a dead snag when I jumped. How long he had been standing there behind me I had no idea.

"We ought not to be here, either one of us," he said. "Some things are just between a man and himself."

"Lucinda Blackburn," Brother Bois said, drawing our attention again to the yard, "I baptize thee in the name of the Father and the Son and the Holy Ghost."

We watched again as he tilted the log, stopped it and began to strain upward, grunting in his effort. And suddenly I was seeing something else—a transfiguration. Not a crabby, over-particular beanpole of a preacher acting the fool with an oak log, but an indomitable spirit, struggling up out of the poor imperfection which beset him toward the Good and Perfect and Divine which beckoned. And not a log with stumps of limbs sticking out like arms, but a cross. And he bearing it, groaning toward Golgotha. It was beautiful and terrible. Then it was gone. I had caught only a glimpse, but that was enough. Too much.

"I'm going," I said to Mr. Hayes.

He looked hard at me, then without a word, turned and led the way. Before we were out of earshot we heard Brother Bois say, "A-men." I could tell by the tone he had failed again, but I knew he would keep trying.

The day of Lucinda's baptism broke fair, but as Mrs. The-obold and I were walking back to the store after the morning worship service, we could see big white clouds beginning to build. "It would be a shame if it rained and ruined it," she remarked.

Mr. Hayes had the table set and was waiting on us. He was freshly shaved and combed and had on his good clothes.

"Don't tell me you're going," I said.

"And why not?" he said. "It's public. Besides, it's my land."

We hurried through dinner, and by one-thirty we were there, and I was holding the car door open for Mrs. Theobold to climb out of the back seat. We were not the first, or even close to it. Cars and trucks and wagons and teams had left the road and crossed the field and already filled all the shady spots under the trees bordering the creek bank. We and those who came after us had to park in the sun.

We made our way through the trees to the creek bank, Mrs. Theobold picking her way carefully, stepping high so as not to dirty her good shoes. The crowd had formed itself into clumps according to age and interest. There were clumps of men and of women, of serious boys and giggling girls. And ripping and romping and running among them all and in and out of the trees and bushes were streams of little ones. The Blackburns were in a clump to themselves back some distance from the water clustered around Lucinda. They were all talking to her, and she looked scared. Brother Bois, black suit and Bible, was by himself at the water's edge staring out over the creek. He had his back to us, so I couldn't tell how he looked.

"I'll just step over and speak to Mrs. Blackburn," Mrs. Theobold said, and Mr. Hayes and I wandered over and joined a clump of our regulars at the store.

"I'll bet even money he'll never get her under," somebody was saying.

"Here, now!" somebody else said, "This ain't something to be a-betting on. This is the Lord's business. Where's your respect?"

"Aw, I didn't mean actual betting and you know it. What I'm saying is I don't think he can do it. What do you think, Mr. Hayes?"

"Leave me out of this," Mr. Hayes said.

"I'll tell you what," another one of them said, "if he don't get started pretty soon, he's going to be doing it in a downpour. It's rain in that cloud yonder, you just mark my words."

We all looked. The cloud was big and had a high top and a black bottom, but it was still some distance away.

"That's what Rile told him a few minutes ago."

"What'd he say?"

"He said it was announced for two o'clock and two o'clock it was going to be."

"I could have told you that."

"Well, what does he care? He's going to be wet anyway."

"What about the rest of us? What about the women and children? He ought to think about them."

We moved on, Mr. Hayes and I, spoke to several others and finally joined the Blackburns.

"I'm worried about that rain," Rile said.

"It ain't rain I'm worried about," Lucinda said.

"Now Lucinder, honey," Amos said, "it ain't nothing to

it. Just shut your eyes and hold your nose and do like he tells you."

"That's easy enough for you to say. You ain't skeered of water like me."

"Well, you got nobody but yourself to blame," Mrs. Blackburn said. "If you had joined the right church to begin with, all this would of already been taken care of."

We talked on for a while, and then Rile, who had been keeping one eye on Brother Bois and the other on the weather, broke in and said, "Well, finally! He's taking off his coat."

"Oh, Lordy!" Lucinda said.

"Aw, hells bells, Lucinder!" Amos said.

"Now, you just watch your mouth, young mister!" Mrs. Blackburn warned him.

Brother Bois took his time folding up his coat and placing it and his Bible just so on a patch of grass a little way up the bank. Then he picked up a long stake he had cut and had there ready and stepped back down the bank and into the water. By this time most of the others had noticed him and stopped talking, and there was a lot of shushing of the little ones. Now we could hear the low grumble of thunder in the distance, though the sun was still shining where we were.

The creek was running fresh. Zions Cause had been blessed with an unusual amount of rain that summer, a downpour just the day before, so the current was fairly strong, but we were on the inside of the bend and it tended to hug the far bank.

Brother Bois edged on out into the water using the stake to feel the bottom before taking each step. When the water was up past his waist, Mr. Hayes said, "That's probably wise."

"What is?" I asked.

"Getting out where it's deep enough that he won't have to lay her back so far." I guess he was thinking about the trouble Brother Bois had had with that log. "Looks like he's worked it out pretty good."

"There's a big drop-off out there somewhere," I said. I knew that spot in the creek well. I should. I had swum there often enough.

Brother Bois found the drop-off with the next stab. That stake must have been seven or eight feet long, and it went all the way out of sight. Brother took a step backward, stabbed and found bottom again. He left the stake standing there stuck in the bottom mud, fished a white handkerchief out of his pocket and began tying it to the stake.

"Oh, Lordy!" Lucinda said.

We had moved a little way off from the Blackburns, Mr. Hayes and I, but not quite out of earshot.

"It's all right," Amos told her. "Just make sure you stay this side of that stake, that's all."

Brother Bois finished with the handkerchief and moved back toward us until he was about waist-deep in the water. With his shirt wet and sticking to him, you could tell just how skinny he was. Then he raised both hands and began.

He spoke about the rite of baptism, how it and the Lord's Supper were the only rites given to the church. He spoke of the significance of baptism, how it symbolized the burial and resurrection of the Lord. He spoke of the Lord's own baptism and how He commanded the Disciples to go forth and baptize in His name. And as he spoke, the air suddenly darkened. We all looked up, even Brother Bois, to find the cloud had finally covered us.

"Yes, well, I see we must hurry right along," he said but went on with his sermon at the same pace as the air grew darker.

Finally, he finished. "Now let us sing a hymn," he said.

"Hymn!" Rile said. He had edged over close to us. "Hymn! We ain't got time for no hymn!"

"And as we sing," Brother Bois continued, "let the candidate come forward."

"Oh, Lordy!" Lucinda said.

Brother Bois got us started on "Gather at the River." He had a good ear and pitched it so it wasn't too hard to hit the highs and lows if you had any range at all. Amos took Lucinda's arm and led her down to the water where she stopped and they had a short discussion which we couldn't hear because of the singing. Then Lucinda took off her shoes and handed them to Amos and went on alone.

Somebody, Mrs. Blackburn or somebody, ought to have warned her about her dress, although maybe there is nothing to be done about it even if you are forewarned. Air gets trapped under it and it's going to float regardless. Push it down in one place and up it pops in another, as Lucinda discovered. But, as Mr. Hayes observed later, fighting to preserve her modesty kept her mind off her fear of water until she reached Brother Bois, who was waiting with outstretched hand to receive her. He put his arm across her shoulder and led her on out to the stake. When he turned her around to face us, the water came exactly to her armpits, which was where, I suppose, Brother Bois wanted it to be.

While this was going on, the singing had dwindled as one after another dropped out and now it stopped altogether. The air had grown even darker. There was not a breath of a breeze. As we watched, we saw the stake lean with the current, come free of the bottom and float away.

"There it goes!" several whispered. If Brother Bois saw it, he didn't bother trying to catch it. He was busy arranging hands—Lucinda's left gripping her right wrist, his left covering her right—and getting into position to her left and slightly behind her and getting his feet set to suit him. Still, he wasn't satisfied. Maybe the bottom was too soft. He looked right and left, took them back a step and went through it again. Finally, he got it right and raised his right hand over her head.

"Lucinda Blackburn," he said. "I baptize thee in the name of the Father and the Son and the Holy Ghost!"

He brought his right hand down and placed it on the back of her neck; his left hand holding hers he brought up and covered her nose and mouth. Then he laid her back. It was total immersion—for a fraction of a second. Then both her feet broke the surface. As Herman Poser had taken the trouble to tell us, fat people float, so when Brother Bois pushed her down at one end, the other end had to rise.

I guess when Brother Bois saw those feet pop up, the dismay must have paralyzed him, because he continued to hold her head down. And Lucinda must have panicked, because those feet began to kick—like she was pedaling a bicycle in a hurry, somebody described it later, or stomping a snake—and her arms came free and began to thrash the water. And still Brother Bois was paralyzed, until one of those big arms caught him across the chest and knocked him loose and out into the creek where he disappeared in deep water. And then we realized the significance of Herman's other point.

Lucinda came to the surface then, all of her, arms flailing, legs pumping, and though she didn't know it, doing a pretty effective back stroke, which took her out into deep water, too. With all that pumping and kicking, her dress was riding up around her waist and we could see her underwear.

"Lord-a-mercy, she's showing everything she's got!" Mrs. Blackburn said. "Rile! Amos! Do something!" But they were frozen to the spot as we all were.

About that time, Brother Bois popped up beside Lucinda. I could tell by the way he was pawing the water he couldn't swim. I guess Mr. Hayes could, too, because he hollered, "Come on, let's go!"

He took a step or two, then stopped and hollered, "Shoes!" We both bent down and began untying our shoes because nobody is going to do any strong swimming with shoes on. I got mine off right away, but one of his laces had wound up in a hard knot and he was yanking on it, trying to break it.

Brother Bois had now noticed Lucinda and grabbed a handful of her dress and tried to pull himself up out of the water. In the process he managed to roll her over on her belly. Some claimed later she didn't miss a beat, just kept on windmilling and kicking. Mrs. Blackburn had been wrong about her showing everything. Now we could see parts we hadn't been able to before.

Mr. Hayes despaired of ever getting his other shoe off and hollered, "Hell with it! Come on!" And he began hopping down the bank to the water.

He never reached it. With a blinding flash and an earsplitting bang, the heavens opened up and deluged us all. The rain! You couldn't see through it or hear above its roar. All you could do was try to find something to hang on to and hope you wouldn't drown or get washed away.

I don't know how long it lasted. Not long, else it would have flooded the whole country. When it slacked off and I could see again, I was looking at disaster. People in a daze, sitting or sprawled in the mud. Clothes soaked and sticking to the flesh. Straw hats with brims drooping and falling apart. Hair plastered to the scalp, matted or hanging down in strings. Mr. Hayes was on all fours, trying to climb back up the bank, having forgotten for the moment, I guess, what he was about. You couldn't tell which foot had the shoe on it, they were both so covered in mud. Mrs. Blackburn was sitting on the ground staring at nothing, unaware I'm sure that her dress was hiked up above her knees. Amos was up on one knee beside her, looking down the creek. "Buck him, Lucinder!" he hollered. "Buck him a good one!"

I looked where he was looking and there they were. Lucinda still had her arms and legs going, her big bottom riding high in the water. And Brother Bois was astride her, one hand clutching her dress at the back of her neck and the other waving around in the air to maintain his balance, looking for all the world like a bull rider in a rodeo. The current had them and was moving them along at a pretty good clip.

"Buck him, Lucinder!" Amos hollered again. "Why don't you buck him?"

If Lucinda heard, she didn't answer or buck either. She just kept on thrashing until she and Brother Bois swung around the bend and passed from our sight.

I was still staring at where they had disappeared when Mr. Hayes came scrabbling up the bank and ruined his other shoe by stomping his muddy foot into it. "Come on, everybody!" he hollered. "We can cut across and catch them!"

We caught her but not him. Well, if you want to be precise about it, we didn't catch her, a sand bar did. She had drifted onto it and was sitting there high and dry when we found her. Mr. Hayes and I got to her a little ahead of the rest because we had left earliest.

"Where's Brother Bois?" Mr. Hayes hollered, but she wasn't in any shape to answer. Not from the water—she had been too buoyant for that to be a problem—but she was on the verge of hysterics. She was holding herself and rocking and going "Oh, Lordy!" over and over.

But Brother Bois was all right, at least he was alive and kicking, because we could see his tracks leading off the sand bar and into the woods. Then the others arrived and scuffed them out.

We saw Brother Bois again, Mr. Hayes and I, late that night. We were just going to bed, Mrs. Theobold had long since done so, when he knocked on the store door. He and Mr. Hayes stood on the store porch and talked, I just inside the door where I could hear.

"I've brought the keys," he told Mr. Hayes.

"It wasn't your fault," Mr. Hayes said. "You did everything you could."

"Could wasn't good enough."

"You did baptize her."

"Yeah, I guess that's something to be thankful for, anyhow."

There was silence for a moment, and then Mr. Hayes asked, "What will you do? Where will you go?"

"I don't know. Maybe back to keeping books. I done that well."

"Seems a shame," Mr. Hayes said.

There was another stretch of silence, and then Brother Bois said, "Tell them I'm—regretful." And then he left.

"Maybe it's just as well," Mr. Hayes said when he was gone. "If it hadn't been this, it would have been something else. You can never be perfect."

I thought of that glimpse I had caught from the locust thicket back of the parsonage and decided there was something mighty noble in trying, though.

A Feast of Onions
[1932]

It had been snowing most of the day. By dusk, we had six
inches on the ground, and it was still falling, heavy enough at
times to blot out the far side of the road in front of the store.
We were alone, Mr. Hayes and I, those who had whiled away
the afternoon with us having left to beat the dark home. The
last to leave was Big Jack Heddin, who only had to go across
the road and down a ways to his living quarters behind his
blacksmith shop, which since autmobiles had become more
prevalent in Zions Cause doubled as a service and repair station, too.

Big Jack, like so many large men, had a gentle and even-
tempered nature, a fact that was unacceptable to most of Zions
Cause, who insisted that reality should coincide with appearance, which in Big Jack's case was formidable. So mention
was often made how once Big Jack dropped a mule with his
bare fist, which was essentially true, except it wasn't really a
mule but a colt that had been brought him to shoe. In the process, the colt had somehow got its left hind leg tangled up with

a hot horseshoe and in the thrashing and kicking which followed was in danger of splitting open the skull of the boy who had brought it and was standing way too close observing the operation. It was true that Big Jack hit the colt between the eyes and felled it. It was also true, though invariably ignored, that even before the animal had time to come to its senses, Big Jack was down beside it cooing over it and applying a soothing salve to its burns.

They were also quick to tell about the time Big Jack caught Ish Theobold with an uppercut, turning him over in a somersault and some claiming adding six inches to his height. True again, at least true that Big Jack hit him and knocked him senseless, but it was in regret rather than anger. What was obvious to those who were there and witnessed it was that nothing less would have satisfied Ish, who had taken offense at some remark Big Jack was only rumored to have made concerning Mrs. Theobold and was hellbent on satisfaction on the field of honor, so to speak.

So by carefully culling the evidence, they managed to carry on the fiction that Big Jack was a man of violence. "He may act easygoing," they would tell one another, "but don't never get him mad. Let him get on a rampage and there ain't no stopping him."

Big Jack had been dragging for several days, complaining of aches and weakness and of being either too hot or too cold, all of which sounded to Mr. Hayes mighty like the onset of the flu. "And when Big Jack is sick," Mr. Hayes said as we stood at the front windows and watched him disappear into the snow, "it comes very close to constituting an epidemic."

The business day of the store was obviously over so we

set about cleaning up, using this to help fill the time before Mrs. Theobold would call us to supper, which smelled to us almost ready. I swept up and Mr. Hayes stoked the stove and emptied the cash register. We finished just ahead of supper. Mr. Hayes had gone to the front windows for another check on the weather when Mrs. Theobold came in from the back to tell us it was ready.

"Now, where do you reckon she's headed?" Mr. Hayes said. He had his hands cupped against the glass, peering out.

"Who?" Mrs. Theobold asked.

"Well, I might be wrong, it's snowing pretty hard and I just caught a glimpse, but it looked like Miss Maggie. What would she be doing out on a night like this?"

Margaret Bumpus, Miss Maggie as she was called, was herb doctor to Zions Cause. She lived alone in a neat little house about a mile or so down the River road, her husband having been gone some twenty years. "Dosed to death over a hangnail," Mr. Hayes said. Nevertheless, the store carried a stock of Miss Maggie's Healing Salve in flat round tins as well as an ample supply of bottles of her All Purpose Tonic, a vile black brew that Mrs. Theobold forced on me at the onset of spring each year to thin the blood. These general nostrums were in chronic demand, but most of Miss Maggie's business was done in specifics. Whatever the ailment, be it carbuncles or gallstones, she would set out to tailor a cure, successfully more often than not—at least the sufferer eventually recovered.

Miss Maggie was visible everywhere in Zions Cause. In all seasons she could be seen stepping briskly along, dressed in decent black even to her wide-brimmed hat, with a split market basket in one hand and a hickory stave in the other, bent on collecting herbs and roots and Lord knows what for her nostrums or delivering the finished product to one of her patients. She was much respected for her contribution to the health of the community, in fact several claimed to owe their very lives to her, and by virtue of her faithful attendance, she was generally counted as a pillar of the church, but there were those in Zions Cause who would whisper behind their hands that there was a dark side to Miss Maggie. Why else did she insist on such secrecy when concocting her remedies, and in the dead of night, too? And when you saw her lights burning way after bedtime, if you got up close enough, you could hear mumbling and mouthing, but not be able to make out a word. Now, what else would that be but spells and incantations and the like? No, it was very much feared that Mistress Maggie Bumpus, despite her standing in the community, might just be tainted with a touch of the black, maybe even to the point of dalliance with Old Scratch himself. To which Mr. Hayes replied that secrecy was surely a necessity, because if anybody knew what went into her stuff they would never be able to swallow it or keep it down if they did, and that all that mumbling was more than likely just her asking the good Lord for forgiveness for inflicting it on them.

"On a mission of mercy, if it was her," Mr. Hayes said as we went in to supper.

"Well, she had to come out anyway," Mrs. Theobold said, which was true. It was Wednesday, and Miss Maggie was almost as faithful in attendance at the weekly prayer service as Mrs. Theobold herself, who was already dressed for the occasion, all but her hat, and snow or no snow would be leaving as soon as supper was finished. Actually, she didn't have all that far to go; the church stood only a quarter of a mile from the store.

After Mr. Hayes and I cleared the supper table and washed the dishes, which by unspoken agreement we did on Wednesday and Sunday evenings to free Mrs. Theobold for church, we spent a drowsy hour in our sitting room, shoes off, feet propped up close to the stove, reading and dozing. By eight-thirty I was about ready to give it up. Mr. Hayes had already done so, his book lying flat on his chest, head back, mouth open, dead to the world. I tiptoed into the store to fix the fire there for the night and then went on to the front windows for a last look at the weather before turning in. The snow had finally stopped. The sky had cleared, and the moon was out.

Standing there in the warmth of the store looking out at the fresh fallen snow, I was infused with a sense of comfort and security, a feeling of smugness, almost arrogance, which seemed to say, *I am here, ha, ha, and you can't touch me.* The world outside had become strange and wondrous, without edges, just swoops and swirls, mounds and hollows; and shapes, softened by flow and fusion, had become almost unrecognizable. And all was new, untouched and untainted. But not for long.

Maybe I heard the door of the blacksmith shop bang open. Or maybe I caught a flash of movement out of the corner of my eye. Whatever drew my attention, when I looked there was Big Jack in just his longjohns in a dead run toward the store, setting off puffs of snow every time a foot hit, and picking up speed as he came on. I must have hollered, for I heard Mr. Hayes answer from the sitting room, but I couldn't answer back because I was too busy trying to get the door, which had frozen shut, open to let Big Jack in when he got there. I still didn't have it open when Mr. Hayes came running in wanting to know what the devil the matter was. He saw what I was trying to do and lent his weight to mine, and between the two of us we finally broke it loose and yanked it open—just in time to see Big Jack pass. He wasn't coming to the store; he didn't even look our way. He was pumping down the middle of the road, throwing snow in all directions, neck thrust forward, hair flying, headed for parts unknown, at least to us. And the moonlight had fooled me. He wasn't wearing longjohns. He was as naked as the day he was born.

Mr. Hayes turned to me. His mouth was open and working but nothing came out. He tried again, then gave up and motioned toward the road. We went tearing through the door and across the porch, not bothering with the steps, and landed in deep snow in front of the store. We were too late to catch Big Jack. But he had left a trail a blind man could follow.

"Shoes!" Mr. Hayes hollered.

I wondered what in the world he was talking about and then realized that we were both in stocking feet. We dashed back in, using the steps this time and stopping briefly on the store porch to knock some of the snow off our feet and legs. We stomped into our shoes, grabbed our hats and coats and were making for the door when Mr. Hayes stopped and hollered, "Blanket!" Well, Big Jack was going to need one if we ever caught up with him. He whirled and ran back to get one and caught up again about the time I reached the road.

Big Jack had kicked out a nice path for us, so we would be able to make good time, but we soon found out we didn't have far to go because we could see that the tracks turned in at the

church. And then we began to hear the hollering coming
through the open door. I guess Big Jack hadn't bothered to
turn the knob, just hit the panel with his shoulder or maybe
his fist and splintered the jamb.

Electric power had not yet come to Zions Cause, so the
church used kerosene lamps, which were set on little shelves
spaced around the walls. Only those toward the front had been
lit, because that was where the few—mostly women—who
had turned out for the prayer service were, and in the dim
light it was hard for us to make out what was happening. There
was a confusion of screeching, but out of it all we could recognize Mrs. Theobold hollering, "Good Lord!" and maybe Mr.
Billy Gusto hollering, "Here, now!" and surely Rile Blackburn hollering, "God damn it, Jack!" They were all in a bunch
moiling around Big Jack, whose head was sticking up in the
center. All, that is, except Brother Sam Sizemore, the pastor.
He was standing in the pulpit looking down on it all, as if he
were waiting for things to settle down so he could get on with
the service.

As we started down the aisle to the front, Mrs. Blackburn,
who could still tip a scale at two hundred easily, came stagger-
ing backward out of the crowd waving her arms and sat down
on the floor hard enough that we could feel the jar. Then here
came Mr. Billy backpedaling out. He just might have kept his
balance had he not stumbled over Mrs. Blackburn. Rile didn't
have a chance; he was airborne from the first. He had untangled himself from Mrs. Blackburn and Mr. Billy and was
getting to his feet when we reached them. He yelled at Mr.
Hayes to help pin him, and together they charged in through
the gap Rile had made on his way out and grabbed Big Jack by

the arms, one on each side. I could see the muscles in Big Jack's back begin to knot, the cheeks of his rump tighten. Then he slowly raised his arms, and Mr. Hayes' and Rile's feet left the floor. At that point my view was blocked as Mrs. Theobold filled the gap. She had a stick of stovewood raised above her head.

"Now, sir!" she said and brought it down. There was a loud crack. She stepped calmly back out of the way. Then everything stopped and we waited. Finally, Big Jack began to fall. Not collapse but fall, full length, like a tree. He fell backward bringing Mr. Hayes and Rile down with him. Then everything stopped again.

Mrs. Theobold had the best view of Big Jack as he lay sprawled on the floor, his outstretched arms pinning down Mr. Hayes and Rile, utterly exposed. In the silence her eyes drifted slowly down the length of his body and then started back up. "Good Lord!" she whispered as if in disbelief.

Then it all started up again. Mr. Hayes and Rile began to free themselves and get up. The crowd began pushing and shoving to get a better look at Big Jack, those in front telling those in back, "Don't look! Don't look!"

Especially they tried to keep away Sister Grace, the pastor's wife, two or three of the women trying without success to prevent her. Briefly she appeared at the front of the crowd, her hands clutching the front of her dress, her eyes red-rimmed and staring, her mouth open and gaping, before she was jerked away.

Mr. Hayes finally ended it, located the blanket he had brought and dropped when he went in to help Rile, and covered Big Jack's nakedness. And then we could get down to the business of seeing how much damage Mrs. Theobold had done with that stick of stovewood, which she still carried in her hand. Mr. Hayes knelt and examined the back of Big Jack's head, taking some time over it.

"Do you think I hit him too hard?" Mrs. Theobold asked him.

"Hard enough. It broke the skin some and raised a knot the size of my fist, but I reckon he will live, though he may be sorry. He's going to have a hell of a headache for the next day or two. Now, don't worry about it, it had to be done. The thing now is to get him home where he can be looked after."

"Is that more important than getting her home so she can be looked after?" Brother Sam said. He had not moved from the pulpit where we had first seen him.

"Who?" Mr. Hayes asked him.

"My wife Grace."

"What's the matter with her?"

"Who do you think he was after?"

It had not occurred to me, I guess it hadn't had time, that Big Jack was after anything. And if it had, the last thing I would have expected would have been a woman. Why, he was shy around men; he could hardly bring himself to speak to a woman. And if it was a woman he was after, the last one I would have expected it to be would have been Sister Grace Sizemore. Granted she was in his age range, maybe a year or so older, thirty maybe. But she was plain, almost drab, and small, scarcely larger than a child. In fact, that's what she looked like, a skinny, flat-chested, narrow-hipped twelve- or thirteen-year-old, with a woman's dress hung on her. Maybe if she had worn her hair in some other way, cut short maybe and curled instead of hanging straight down her back, or maybe used a touch of make-up to relieve the flatness of her features, it would have helped. But of course she was the pastor's wife and those options would not have been open to her. And that, too—she was the pastor's wife; that alone, if nothing else had, should have put him off. And who would have thought of him sitting there Sunday after Sunday under the drone of Brother Sam's interminable sermons, watching her where she sat in the choir, looking at her and nursing a secret lust? And who, by any stretch of the imagination, would ever have dreamed that he would act on that lust?

Later, when I said all this to Mr. Hayes, he pointed out something I had missed about Sister Grace, missed because at twelve years old I was not yet able to perceive it, springing from the very quality that I had decried. Where I had despised her childish appearance, her undeveloped body, at a later age I might have been aroused, stirred as Big Jack had been, and presumably Mr. Hayes too, by the illusion she projected of virginal purity. For me it was an early glimpse of one of the baser aspects of human nature, that urge to violate, to destroy, innocence.

Sister Grace, as it turned out, was the first to be taken care of. She was led off up the aisle in the charge of Mrs. Blackburn and three or four of the other women, calm, erect, eyes straight ahead, as if in a daze. Brother Sam followed a few paces behind. They wouldn't have far to go; the parsonage was just next door.

Providing for Big Jack presented a problem, though. There were not enough of us to carry him home, and even if there had been, it would have been difficult with the snow. So we had to use Mr. Billy's car, bundling him into the back seat with

Mr. Hayes on one side and Rile on the other. Mrs. Theobold and I rode up front with Mr. Billy. Mr. Hayes told Mr. Billy to just stop at the store, that we would keep him for a while, which seemed to please Mrs. Theobold, who was still feeling guilty.

"What in the world do you reckon got into him?" Rile asked.

"Good question," Mr. Hayes said. "What happened exactly?"

All three of them tried to tell it at once, interrupting and correcting each other and arguing over details. They had all been huddled in the first few pews on the right side of the aisle because the stove sat in that corner. Rile was on the aisle in the first pew. Mrs. Blackburn was next to him, then Sister Grace, then Mr. Billy and the other Gustos. The service was just about over, Brother Sam well into his benediction and all heads bowed, when the door flew open. They thought it was the wind until they heard bare feet slapping the floor, so by the time they looked up, Big Jack was already on them. He went past Rile and Mrs. Blackburn, straight to Sister Grace, and took her under the arms and lifted her out of her seat. He may or may not have called her by name. Mrs. Blackburn and Mr. Billy, who were the closest, grabbed his arms. He let go of Sister Grace to fling them off. Then Rile tried to grab him. By that time some of the others had got there and were hitting at him with hymnals and purses. Mrs. Theobold, who had been in the second pew next to the wall, picked up a stick of wood from the stack next to the stove as she passed and was circling around waiting for an opening when we came in.

"It was her and only her he was after, I'm satisfied of that," Mr. Billy said, "and there's not much question, either, as to what he had on his mind."

"Good Lord! He didn't have nothing on his mind," Mrs. Theobold said. "He was clean out of his mind, you could tell that by the way his eyes was set. Good Lord!"

"Well, I never took notice of his eyes," Mr. Billy said, "and I wish now I had never grabbed him by the arm. I may not be able to move for a month."

By the time we got to the store, Big Jack was beginning to come around and was able with the help of Mr. Hayes and Rile to stumble in. Mrs. Theobold ran on ahead to fix up the sitting room couch for him, and before we even had him stretched out on it, she had already brought warm water and bandages. She shoved us out of the way and set about bathing the wound and cleaning the blood out of his hair, stopping now and then to whisper to herself, "Good Lord!" And Big Jack would groan occasionally as if in reply, but he was far from being rational yet.

"Time and rest," Mr. Hayes said. "That's what it's going to take."

So Mr. Billy and Rile left to go back to the church so Mr. Billy could collect Mrs. Gusto and the girls and Rile could take Mrs. Blackburn home. And Mr. Hayes and I slipped out to go across to Big Jack's place to see if we could find some clothes for him to put on.

The sky had gone dark again threatening more snow, and the wind had picked up, which made the night a lot colder. We hurried along single file, our heads bowed to the wind, our shoulders hunched up to our ears, trying to keep to Big Jack's tracks. As we turned out of the road into the shop, Mr. Hayes stopped, so suddenly I almost plowed into him.

"What's the matter?" I asked.

"The door is shut."

Well, of course it was shut. What did he expect? Then I understood. The state Big Jack was in, he wouldn't have bothered with the door, certainly hadn't with the one at the church, so how did it get closed?

"Maybe the wind," I said.

"Maybe," he said, but he went on more slowly, peering down at the tracks in the snow. I looked, too, but it was too dark to make out anything except the outlines of the furrow Big Jack had made. He stopped again before we reached the door and bent down to take a closer look. Over his shoulder, I could see what might have been a shoe print, or might not; anyway, at the rate the wind was blowing loose snow around, even Big Jack's tracks were soon going to be drifted over.

Inside the shop it was pitch dark, but we could see a thin line of light at the bottom of the door to Big Jack's living quarters. Maybe the wind had shut that door, too. We groped our way over to it, worried that our path might be blocked with some piece of farm machinery Big Jack had been working on.

The living quarters consisted of one large room, but in it was everything a man would need to live comfortably: a sink under the rear window with a cookstove on one side and a kitchen cabinet on the other; a bed along another wall and a night stand—that's where the lamp was sitting—and a dresser and clothes press; a heating stove in a corner with an easy chair drawn up to it; a bookcase, the top shelf filled with trinkets and curios; an assortment of pictures and samplers and calendars around the walls; and in the center of the room a small kitchen table with two cane-bottom straight chairs. Everything was in perfect order as if it had just been tidied up, even the bed was made, and the whole place smelled of onions, cooked onions.

The smell of onions was not remarkable. It was well known that Big Jack was a fool over them. He ate them like apples, polishing off eight or ten at a sitting. He ate them in sandwiches. He ate them fried, baked or boiled. He could make an entire meal, and often did when he could get them, off onions alone, and it would appear he had just done so again. What was remarkable was, considering the state he must have been in, that he would have gone to the trouble of removing all traces of the meal, except the smell, of course; there wasn't much he could have done about that.

When I mentioned this to Mr. Hayes, he said, "Well, that wasn't the only thing he took care of. Look around. Do you see any sign of the clothes he took off? I'll bet anything we'll find them hanging in that clothes press."

He was not a hundred percent right. Big Jack's longjohns we found in the dirty clothes hamper.

The next morning we moved Big Jack from the sitting room couch, which was too short for him anyway, to my room, which was not only more comfortable but quieter, because, as Mr. Hayes had predicted, his head was causing him acute distress. He was rational now, but that stick of stovewood had messed up his memory somewhat. He was in considerable confusion about the events of the past several days; of the previous night, he remembered nothing. Mr. Hayes had been right about something else, too. On top of his other ailments, Big Jack had a touch of the flu and was alternately sweating and chilling. And he would be lucky, in Mrs. Theobold's opinion, if he didn't take pneumonia as well.

We were busy at the store that day. The challenge of the snow alone would have been enough to bring them out—after all, the surest way to satisfy yourself that you are not snow-bound is to go somewhere—but there was the additional need to discuss Big Jack's abortive assault on Sister Grace, which most of them had only heard about and second- or third-hand at that.

They say he was falling-down drunk.

Well, he wasn't.

From what I hear Rile Blackburn was the one that done the falling down, him and Mr. Hayes.

Now, don't slight Mr. Billy Gusto and Mrs. Blackburn. They done their share, too, so I'm told.

Big Jack don't drink. I've never known him to touch a drop, and nobody else has, neither.

Well, then, I reckon he ain't got no excuse. Anyway, I hear Brother Sam is going to turn him out of the church.

He can't do that. The whole congregation would have to vote him out.

Well, if Brother Sam wants it, he's got my vote. If it had been my wife, I would of shot the son of a bitch.

I wouldn't say that around where Big Jack might hear me if I was you, not unless I had Mrs. Theobold behind him with a stick of stovewood.

And so it went all day long. The membership changed from time to time, but the central issue remained the same. And as the day wore on, it seemed that more and more of them were drifting to Brother Sam's side.

"So what if they do turn him out," I said to Mr. Hayes that night after they had all gone, "what does it amount to? Just that he can't take the Sacrament or vote on church business. And what's so special about that? You've got along without it all these years, and it sure hasn't bothered me."

"It amounts to something more than that," he told me. "I, and so far you, for whatever reason have chosen not to belong. Big Jack made the opposite choice. It's something he wants, something maybe he needs and certainly something he sees as good and right. If they turn him out, it will be his friends and neighbors saying he is no longer fit for fellowship with them, that they condemn and reject him. And all over something he can't even remember, may never be able to, so he won't even have the knowledge of guilt to help him accept it. Maybe it won't be as bad as if they just ganged up and stoned him to death, but to a man like Big Jack, it will come mighty close."

Friday, the store was full again. Opinions had more or less solidified. It was definite now that at the close of the Sunday morning worship service Brother Sam was going to bring charges against Big Jack, and it appeared that there would be enough votes to turn him out of the church.

Rile and two or three others stopped by to inquire about Big Jack and see if there was anything they could do to help. They stepped in to speak to him, but he was too sick to do much more than shake hands. It wasn't his head that was bothering him so much now; it was the flu.

By evening he was running a high fever, and we were using cold cloths on his forehead. It was obvious that somebody was going to have to sit up, so we agreed to take shifts. Mrs. Theobold would sit until eleven, then I would be on until three, and Mr. Hayes would finish out the night.

As soon as we had finished clearing away supper, I settled

down on the sitting room couch to get in some sleep before my shift. Mr. Hayes said he was turning in early, too, but I suppose he fell asleep in his chair and missed the opportunity. Anyway, he was still in the sitting room at ten-thirty when Mrs. Theobold woke us to tell us that Big Jack's fever had broken and that he was asleep and probably wouldn't need anything the rest of the night.

"I may as well tell you, though," she said, "he was out of his head for a while and done a lot of talking."

"About what?" he asked.

"Sister Grace," she said, "and Miss Maggie."

Mr. Hayes rose up in his chair. "What about Miss Maggie?"

"Oh, it was all a muddle. I couldn't tell whether the things he was saying was about Sister Grace or Miss Maggie."

"What things!"

"Good Lord! I'm not going to repeat them! Besides, he was clean out of his head."

Saturday morning soon after breakfast Mr. Hayes asked Mrs. Theobold to keep an eye on the store while we made a couple of calls.

"Where are we going?" I asked.

"The parsonage, for one place," he said.

It was said of Brother Sam that he shaved and changed underwear twice daily and put on a fresh shirt before every meal. He was certainly immaculate as he opened the door to us, already fully dressed in white shirt and tie, even wearing a coat and vest with a triangle of white handkerchief sticking out of his breast pocket, and the strands of his thin brown hair carefully arranged to hide his shiny scalp. He peered at us through silver-rimmed spectacles for a moment, then shook hands and invited us in.

Sister Grace, who had been standing behind him, looked at us anxiously, started to speak, then changed her mind.

"What is it, Grace?" Brother Sam asked.

"I was just wondering if they would like some coffee."

"That would be mighty welcome," Mr. Hayes said.

There was something different about her that at first I couldn't place. Then I realized it was her hair. It was pulled back from her face and held by a band of red ribbon. She took our coats, and Brother Sam led us into his study. He spoke briefly about the weather and then asked us our business, but before Mr. Hayes could answer, Sister Grace came in with the coffee and served it.

"That will do fine, Grace," Brother Sam said and waited until she, somewhat reluctantly, I thought, left the room, then said, "Now, Brother Hayes."

"You know why we're here," Mr. Hayes said.

"I expect I do."

"You know, of course, it was not a deliberate act. He was not himself."

"I don't know that, but I'm willing to concede such may have been the case."

"Then, how can you hold him responsible?"

"You are not a Christian, Brother Hayes."

"I'm not a member of the church."

"Exactly. And this is church business. How can it concern you?"

"It's also community business. What you're proposing won't stop at the church door."

"I sincerely hope not."

Brother Sam's smugness was irritating. I could tell it was beginning to get to Mr. Hayes, too.

"But why? You're willing to admit that it wasn't an act of volition. It's unthinkable that in his right mind he, or anybody else in Zions Cause, would behave in such a way. He was coming down with the flu, was probably running a high fever. He simply didn't know what he was doing."

"Ah, but that's the very point you're missing! The evil was there already. It's not so much the act itself that condemns him as the corruption it springs from—his lust for her. And that didn't just happen suddenly and without his having any control over it. No, that is something he knew about, allowed to grow, perhaps fed through fantasies. There is the evil, Brother Hayes, and that's why he must be cast out."

Mr. Hayes thrust forward in his chair. "Good Lord!" he said, "that condemns us all!"

"Not all, Brother Hayes, not all."

Mr. Hayes stared at him for a moment. "Not you, I take it."

"You don't touch pitch, you don't get black."

Mr. Hayes leaned back in his chair. "And you have never touched pitch," he said.

"Never."

"And Sister Grace?"

"Never."

They sat there for a time staring at each other, Brother Sam with a faint smile on his face. Then Mr. Hayes said, "But now it may be she has been touched."

Brother Sam's smile faded. "What do you mean?" he asked.

"She knows it was her he chose and for what purpose. And she has seen him, all of him. Can she close her mind to that?"

"She will resist it. I will see to it."

"And even if you manage to get him turned out, he will still be here, physically here. She will have to see him, and she will remember."

Now Brother Sam thrust forward in his chair, his eyes wide behind his spectacles. "No! She will not!"

"And you. Why was it you never left the pulpit, never tried to stop it? Was it because a part of you wanted it to happen, wanted to watch it? Could it be that you've been touched, too?"

Brother Sam jumped to his feet, shouting, "No! Stop! Enough!"

A movement in the doorway caught my eye. It was Sister Grace. I wondered how long she had been standing there. Maybe Brother Sam did, too. He calmed himself and said, "This discussion is ended. I'll get your coats."

He brushed by Sister Grace and left the room. She looked back and forth between Mr. Hayes and me a time or two and then chose me. "How is he?" she whispered.

"He's fine," I whispered back. Then Brother Sam was there with our coats.

When we were in the car, I said, "I'm not real sure I understood all that went on in there."

"I'm not sure I did either," he said. "But maybe, just maybe I might have got lucky."

"You told Mrs. Theobold two calls," I said. "Is the other one Miss Maggie?"

"You know, you're getting to be about half smart," he said and started the car.

We had just been invited out of one place, and it looked for a minute as if we wouldn't even get invited in at the second.

"I can't give you long," Miss Maggie told us. "There are things I need to be doing."

"This won't take you long," Mr. Hayes told her, and he surely didn't waste any time getting to it. "Just what did you give him?"

"Give who?"

"Surely you realize we wouldn't be here if we didn't know most of it already."

"Well, it was just a dish of boiled onions, if you must know."

"But you put a little something in with the onions, didn't you?"

"He was coming down with the flu."

"What was it?"

"I can't see that's anybody's business but mine."

"Good Lord, woman! Here a decent, gentle, upstanding member of the community, who wouldn't harm a fly, runs wild, tracks stark naked through the snow in twenty-degree weather, busts down the door of the church and tries to assault the preacher's wife in the middle of a prayer meeting, winds up with his head split open and a concussion, and now is likely to be disgraced for life, and you've got the gall to claim it's nobody's business but yours. Nobody's fault but yours is more like it!"

"Well, I never meant—how could I know it would take him like that?"

"What would take him like that? What in God's name was it?"

"A love potion."

"What!"

"I didn't follow the directions exactly, I admit that. I added some things I thought would make it stronger. But I said all the words right, I was careful to do that. He didn't want to let me in until I showed him the onions and raised the lid and let him smell them. I heated them up, and he finished the whole bowl. I could tell it was beginning to work because he started to act sleepy. I got him to the bed and took off his clothes. That was all I really had in mind, just to look at him, maybe touch him. But it was her he wanted, not me, and I couldn't hold him." Miss Maggie's voice broke. Her face crumpled, and she covered it with her hands.

We waited. It was the silence of her crying that made it so terrible to me. Finally, she said, "I suppose he told you everything."

"No," Mr. Hayes said. "As a matter of fact, he doesn't remember anything about it, either before or after. Only the three of us know."

"It will have to come out, I guess."

"That depends on whether we can be sure that something like this will never happen again."

"You can be sure."

"I believe we can."

On our way home, Mr. Hayes said, "If it ever reached a showdown, it would be just our speculation against her denial. We couldn't offer a shred of evidence."

"What about that shoe print in the snow?"

"I couldn't swear to it, and even if I could, that wouldn't make it hers. Come to that, I couldn't even swear it was her I saw passing in front of the store. No, it was all bluff, and we got more out of it than we could have reasonably expected to. But just watch, she will recover pretty quick when she realizes there's nothing concrete against her. But I expect she will think twice before trying it again."

Sunday morning, despite the deep snow which still covered the ground and the continued low temperature, the church was packed. Mr. Hayes was not there, of course, nor Big Jack—he was well on the mend but still not mobile—however, everybody else seemed to be. Mrs. Theobold and I found seats near the center, so we had a good view. I spotted Miss Maggie in her customary black, half-turned in her seat and carrying on a lively conversation with Mrs. Blackburn and Mrs. Gusto, who were in the pew behind her. As Mr. Hayes had predicted, it hadn't taken her long to recover. The members of the choir began filling the space to the left of the pulpit, among them Sister Grace, but, as I gradually became aware, a new and different Sister Grace, or at least the promise of one. The transformation was not all that obvious. Her hair was drawn back and caught in a bun at the nape of her neck. She had taken some of the slack out of the bodice of her dress so that it fit her now instead of just hanging on her. But the real difference was more subtle. There seemed to be a kind of glow about her, and her mouth bore just a suggestion of a smile.

Brother Sam mounted to the pulpit, combed and creased and polished in his customary manner. When the preliminaries were over, he announced that after the service he would have a very serious matter to lay before the church, which set off a series of mumblings throughout the sanctuary. Then he launched into his sermon, which as always was closely reasoned, supported by innumerable citations, delivered with finicky precision, long and exhausting.

When it was finally over, we rushed through the invitation hymn, and then Brother Sam gave those in the audience who were not members of the church the opportunity to leave if they so desired. We waited. Nobody left.

"So be it," he said, and then kept us waiting again while he took off his spectacles and polished them with his handkerchief. At last, he was ready.

"My brothers and sisters in Christ, the matter I must bring to you today is one over which I have spent long hours on my knees seeking to know God's will. I am convinced, now, of the way He would have me go."

He paused, looked around the congregation. I could see several heads nodding in front of me. I assumed just as many were doing the same behind me.

"It was two years ago last October that you called me to be your pastor, and the Lord laid it on my heart to come. And He has blessed my ministry here."

There were two or three amens.

"As most of you know, my home is in Bethel, Tennessee, which is also the home of Bethel Bible College, where young men are trained for the ministry. I myself am a graduate of Bethel Bible College. Some months ago, the president of the college wrote me and invited me to join his staff as minister and counselor to the student body. Yesterday, under what I believe to be Divine Guidance, I sent him my letter of acceptance. Therefore, I now tender my resignation as pastor of Zions Cause Church and respectfully request this body to accept it."

There were no murmurs, no whispers, no indrawn breaths, no reaction at all but silence, until finally Mr. Billy broke it.

"But Preacher," he said, "what about Jack Heddin?"

"It is my hope," Brother Sam said, "that you will pray, as I shall, that he be restored in mind and body that he may continue to serve the Lord, for we have all, every one of us, sinned and fallen short of the Glory of God."

"But why?" I asked Mr. Hayes, when Mrs. Theobold and I got home and told him what had happened. "Why, when he knew he had the votes, would he just give up and leave like that?"

"For the reason he gave," Mr. Hayes said, "plus maybe for sanitary reasons."

It took several years for his answer to make any sense to me.

Mule Fire
[1934]

"It beat anything ever I saw!" This was John Bumpus who at the time was Jr. Pease's shadow, more or less, and claimed to have actually witnessed it, hollering some on the theory, I suppose, that louder is more convincing. "He just taken his thumbnail and cracked that match under that mule's tail and ay god it went off like a Christmas rocket trailing a streak of blue fire a good ten foot behind!"

"Actually," Jr. Pease said, "it's more like two foot."

"Well, nobody better never do that to no mule of mine," Amos Blackburn said.

"Aw, it don't hurt them none, just livens them up a little," Jr. Pease said.

"I'll tell you what, boys," Mr. Hayes said. "My advice would be to give up beans. If Jr. Pease ever runs out of windy mules, he might just haul off and light one of us."

Well, none of us really believed it. We didn't have to, you see, because John Bumpus being so much under Jr. Pease's spell could not be considered a reliable witness. And a few days later when he talked Jr. Pease into a demonstration that didn't come off we could become confirmed in our disbelief. So the subject was dropped and all but forgotten.

A month passed, maybe two. It was getting along toward dusk, and we had the store porch full. There was a checker game going and most were watching that, because Rile Blackburn had finally talked Mr. Hayes into a game. Rile had beat everybody else until they wouldn't play with him anymore and was suffering, you might say, from Alexander the Great's old complaint. So nobody noticed him come up, that boy of old man Eli Thompson's, but suddenly there he was standing behind Rile, oversized bib overalls hanging from his bare shoulders, his eyes way too big for that little pinched face following the game. He was fifteen or sixteen years old but would have been taken for no more than eleven or twelve.

After a while Mr. Hayes looked up and noticed him there and said, "What can I do for you—Harold, is it?" He knew, as we all did, that he was there on business, since old man Thompson would never have allowed any of them, including his wife, to be anywhere at leisure.

They had come from somewhere down in Tennessee the year before, one jump ahead of the law so rumor had it, and rented a place from Mr. Charlie Ferguson. There were several of them and Harold was the oldest. Old man Thompson was supposed to have beat his landlord half to death with an axe-handle over some trifle or other. Anyway, when Mr. Charlie heard about it, he stopped going by to collect the rent, just waited for old man Thompson to send it to him, if and when he felt like it.

"HE wants a sack of Bull-Durm," he said, his emphasis capitalizing the pronoun as if it might have been the Deity he was referencing.

Rile had Mr. Hayes down to two kings and was on his way to destroying him completely. "I'll get it," I said.

When I came back, it was over, and Rile was trying to talk Mr. Hayes into another game.

"I'm merely foolish," Mr. Hayes said, "not stupid along with it."

I shouldered my way around to where the boy was standing and handed him the sack of tobacco. He took it and passed me the money, the exact amount as I knew it would be, his eyes never leaving the board. Finally, he looked up at Mr. Hayes, licked his lips a time or two and said in a voice so low that I thought nobody could hear but me, "I'll play him."

"What did you say, Harold?" Mr. Hayes said.

"I said I'll play him."

"Well, come on, then," Mr. Hayes said. "Take my place and welcome. I've done had more of this than I can stand."

"You'll be easy on me, won't you, boy?" Rile said. "Remember, I'm all wore out from the struggle I've just had with Mr. Hayes here."

Rile was beat almost from his first move, though he couldn't believe it. And when he finally accepted it, he still had to endure the humiliation of an utter rout in the presence of witnesses whose hearts had been hardened by his own former ruthlessness.

"It looks like old Rile's done found him a new game," Jr. Pease said. "It's called Giveaway."

Everybody laughed.

"Now wait a minute!" Rile said. "Anybody can luck out once. That's why it's always two out of three. We'll do it again and this time I move first." While they were setting up for a new game, Rile said to the boy, "I'll admit you're good. Who taught you to play like that, anyhow?"

"Nobody," the boy said. "I seen a game once and I studied it out."

"Well, you must play with somebody. Some one of your folks maybe."

He looked at Rile as if he was out of his mind. "Oh no," he said, "HE wouldn't allow no checkers." Then he added almost in a whisper, "I play in my head a lot, though."

The second game took a little longer—a little longer, that is, for Rile to discover he was bested again. He was taking more and more time over each move, crouching over the board and mumbling to himself, reluctant to remove his hand from his checkerpiece, hollering "Wait a minute! Wait a minute, now!" And we were all crouched over the board, too, in consummate satisfaction, thinking, "Lo! How are the mighty fallen!" or something to that effect, when all was brought up short—time and tide and anything else with power of motion—by a mighty voice from on high.

"Come out of there, boy!"

It was not loud like thunder, just spoken in a tone that brooked not let nor hindrance. And it was not from Heaven, as we had first imagined, but merely from mule-back. It was in fact old man Eli Thompson. He had pulled that mule up right against the store porch and was sitting there looking down on us—a tall, lean, straight-backed man, dark as a gypsy, with high cheek bones, small deep-set eyes and thin lips set in faint smile.

"Come on out here and get what's coming!"

We looked then at the boy. He had gone white. His face seemed to have grown even smaller and his eyes larger, if such was possible. He didn't move. Maybe he couldn't.

Mr. Hayes tried. "Well, now, Mr. Thompson," he said. "I wouldn't be too hard on Harold. It was probably our fault more than his."

"I'll thank you, Hayes, to stay out of my business!"

Never before in my life—or since, for that matter—had I ever heard anyone refer to Mr. Hayes by his last name only. I had heard some his age call him Jim, a very few, but never simply Hayes. Even I called him Mr. Hayes, and I had lived with him all my life. It was not something he expected or even wanted from me or anyone else, but something we wanted, something we needed to do. Old man Thompson thought to insult Mr. Hayes. He missed it. He insulted the rest of us instead, because it was our honor and our respect—ours because we bestowed it—he was belittling.

"And you can't deny, Hayes," old man Thompson said, "that it is my business and mine alone."

Mr. Hayes could not deny it. Regardless of the fairness of it, both law and custom decreed then, and to a large extent still do, that a man has a right to govern his family as he sees fit.

"All right, now, boy!"

We stood back then and let the boy move through. He did so slowly, like he might have been pulling through waist-deep water, despair in his eyes and the set of his mouth. Old man

Thompson sat motionless, watching him with that set smile again. When he was in striking distance, old man Thompson's hand moved like a snake, slashing him across the face with the long leather reins. But in the act he committed a serious error. The blow overcarried and caught Jr. Pease, who was standing beside the boy, on the shoulder and that broadened the question of whose business it was.

Jr. Pease hollered and set himself to lunge, but old man Thompson was too quick. Maybe he had had practice. Seemingly out of nowhere the knife appeared in his hand. It was almost the size of a butcher knife. His arm shot out bringing the blade within a foot of Jr. Pease's face.

"Take a good look at it, boy," he said, "and then think again."

For a long moment neither of them moved, nor did we, only the mule, shuffling its feet and wrinkling the skin on its back. Finally, Jr. Pease relaxed, moved a few steps down the porch and leaned against a post. If old man Thompson could have left it there, he might have been all right. But he couldn't. I guess everybody needs respect, or what they are willing to settle for in its stead. He continued to sit there, holding out that knife.

"Anybody else?" he said. "Anybody at all?"

Still he sat, waiting. The mule spread his hind legs, hunched slightly.

"I thought not," he said, or at least I think that's what he started to say, but before he could get it out that mule had raised his tail and Jr. Pease had cracked a match under it.

It was exactly as John Bumpus had described it—a Christmas rocket with a blue flame shooting out behind. Lord, was it beautiful!

We all ran out in the road to watch but were too late to see any more. The cloud of dust that mule raised had blotted everything out. But we could hear old man Thompson. When that mule took off he had started one long sustained bellow. It was still going. It sounded like a train whistle fading off in the distance, and that mule's feet hitting the ground was the clicking of the wheels against the rails.

We stood there until the sound had died out completely and the dust had settled. Finally, somebody said, "You reckon he's still on?"

"Well, if he is," somebody else said, "he must be coming up on the river about now. I'd judge that mule was making better than sixty mile an hour."

"I reckon we had better go find out," Mr. Hayes said. "Get the car."

So I brought the car around and they piled in and on. We must have had eight or ten inside and on the running boards and fenders. Amos Blackburn had come in his truck so he took what was left.

"You sure you can drive this thing?" somebody asked, because I was only fourteen.

"He does fine," Mr. Hayes said, "except when he decides to drive in the ditches."

After we had started, Mr. Hayes asked about Harold. He wasn't with us so we assumed he was riding with Amos. Nobody had noticed him since that rocket blasted off.

It was dark enough now that I had switched on the lights. I

guess we would have missed old man Thompson completely had not someone on the running boards heard him holler. I stopped and they went running back looking in the road ditch and found him. He was pretty well skinned up. And he had a broken leg.

"Well, don't just stand there gawking," he said. "Get me out of here and get me to a doctor."

About that time Amos and his bunch arrived. "What's the matter with him?" they asked.

"Broke leg," our bunch said.

"Too bad," Jr. Pease said. He had come with Amos. "Reckon we'll have to shoot him."

"What's the matter with y'all?" old man Thompson said. "Can't you see I'm hurt bad? Ain't nobody going to help me?"

Nobody moved. They just stood there looking at him. Finally, Mr. Hayes said, "Well, come on, boys. Let's see if we can get him into the back seat of the car."

So we took him to the doctor and then took him home and helped them get him inside. He never once inquired about that boy, Harold. Mr. Hayes did of Mrs. Thompson but she hadn't seen him. In fact, I doubt any of them ever saw him again. When they moved away the next spring, owing Mr. Charlie six months back rent, he still hadn't turned up. Rile Blackburn said we ought not to worry about him, that he could make a living anywhere playing checkers.

Jr. Pease was immortalized—as long as any of us lived, we would be telling his story, and maybe our children and their children, too—but not retired. A Sunday afternoon a few weeks later, Amos Blackburn agreed to take a truckload of us swimming. When we were all loaded up, there was Jr. Pease still sitting on the steps of the store porch.

"Ain't you going with us?" somebody asked.

"Naw," he said. "I think I might go down to the pasture and maybe light me a mule."

"Wait!" John Bumpus said, trying to get out of the truck. "I'll go with you!"

The Centaur
[1935]

Odie Poser loved horses, had from the time he was old enough to notice them. And horses loved Odie. Will, his father, used to say that he suspected Odie was half horse himself, not intending or even recognizing the implied slur upon Odie's mother.

Will farmed not only the forty acres that Mr. Billy Gusto had given him when he married Bessie, the plainest of those Gusto girls, but a good part of Mr. Billy's land as well, so the Posers kept half a dozen horses of their own. Will and Bessie had six children, all boys—Odie was the youngest—so it took that many to keep them busy.

In his early years, Odie spent much of his time with the horses when they were not being used in the fields, petting them and talking to them and running and playing with them. According to Will, Odie would have moved in with them, living and sleeping in the barn and just coming to the house for his meals, if Will had allowed it.

By the time he was ten years old, Odie had a speaking acquaintance with every horse in the county and was able to call each of them by name. Nobody was surprised when at no more than thirteen he took over the entire horseshoeing operation at Big Jack Heddin's Garage and Blacksmith Shop, which Big Jack must have been glad to get rid of since he had his hands full just keeping cars and mowing machines and hay-balers going. To the shoeing business, Odie soon added horse doctoring, which it turned out he was good at, too, being able somehow to sense just what was wrong and what to do about it. So if anybody had trouble with machinery, Big Jack was called on to fix it. And if the trouble was with a horse, it was Odie who was sent for.

That was why Mr. Billy sent for him the next morning after he brought that new horse home. Mr. Billy had been to Benton for what was called Trading Day, an affair held once a year so people could bring what they didn't want or need and sell it or swap it for something else they had no desire or use for, and he bought that horse way too cheap. Late in the day he had started home with it tied to the back bumper of that Pierce Arrow touring car he drove. It took him the better part of four hours to make that twenty or so miles. He said part of the time he was running in low gear and all but dragging it, and it hunkered down on its hind quarters and its front feet set, refusing to go; and part of the time he was running in high gear faster than he liked to drive trying his best to stay ahead of it; and the rest of the time he was stopped, cussing it. It was in his judgment half racehorse and half wild mustang, with a goodly portion of purebred stubborn mule slipped in there somewhere. He didn't get home until long after dark, and when he went out to see about it the next morning, he found it in bad shape, skinned and scraped and its mouth torn and, so he claimed, limping on all four legs. So he sent for Odie, not only to doctor it up but to see if he could gentle it a little, because, he said, it was a fine-looking animal when he bought it.

Odie spent the morning out there and came back as put out as anybody had ever seen him. He said he didn't care if Mr. Billy was an old man, and his grandpaw to boot, he ought to be whipped for mistreating a horse that way.

Odie's doctoring paid off, as it almost always did, and that horse began to heal and started getting around better. He wasn't that successful with improving its mental outlook, though. With Odie, it was as gentle as a dove, but it wouldn't let Mr. Billy in the same pen with it. The first time Mr. Billy tried, it reared up and lashed out and came within a hair of splitting his head open like a ripe watermelon with its front hooves; and would have, too, Odie said, if he hadn't got to it and talked it out of it. Thereafter, all Mr. Billy had to do was lay a hand on that lot gate and that horse would explode like a firecracker.

So in a day or two, Mr. Billy came down to Mr. Hayes' store and tried to sell it to them on the porch, admitting that it was a little high spirited but claiming all it needed was a good working to put it right.

"Then why do you want to sell it?" somebody asked. "Why don't you keep it yourself?"

"Aw, I don't need another horse," he told them. "I just bought it on speculation."

Maybe that was true. But everybody had already heard from

Mr. Billy himself what a time he had getting it home and from Odie how it had nearly killed him.

Rile Blackburn said, "I hear that horse is dangerous."

"Dangerous?" Mr. Billy said. "Dangerous? Why, it lets Odie just waller it around any which way. Who said that horse was dangerous?"

Rile said, "All right. I'll tell you what I'll do. We'll go out there, and if you'll lead that horse out of the lot, I'll buy it."

"Now, I'm going to be honest with you, Rile. That horse don't like me. It gets along with Odie just fine, and I expect it would with you or anybody else, but for some reason I seem to upset it. So you can see you've got me in a bind. It's a fine horse, but it won't tolerate me, so I'm willing to let it go for whatever I can get, and whoever gets it, well, I just hope they don't treat me too bad."

Rile, like Mr. Billy, didn't need another horse, but he needed to trim somebody in a trade. So we all went out to Mr. Billy's to see how that horse would take to Rile. It didn't take to him; it took out after him. That horse was on the far side of the lot facing in the other direction when Rile eased the bar off and cracked that gate no more than six inches. He just had time to bang it shut again and ram that bar back in place, but not enough time to take his hand off it, before that horse slammed into it. He said it felt like somebody had hit that bar with a sledge hammer and that the jar numbed him all the way to the elbow.

He jumped back, holding his arm, and looked at that horse, snorting and prancing and circling the lot now like a sentry walking his post in quick time. Then he looked back at that two-story brick house of Mr. Billy's with its white columns in front and at that Pierce Arrow pulled up under the roof of the side entrance and on to that big snow-white barn before he said. "Mr. Billy, even you ain't got enough money to pay me to take that thing off your hands."

About that time, Odie came pumping up on that bicycle of his. He had just heard what Mr. Billy and Rile were trying to do, and he was upset about it. "You ought to know better than to get him excited again. Every muscle in his legs is strained, and he ain't never going to get well if you don't let him alone."

With that, he opened the gate and went in. That horse came over to him and put its head down, and Odie laid an arm across its neck and they strolled over to the far side of the lot, with Odie talking and that horse nodding its head as if in agreement. Odie examined that shoulder that had hit the gate, taking plenty of time about it, and finally came on out again.

"Now he's got another bad bruise to get over," he said to Mr. Billy and Rile. "I just hope you're satisfied."

Mr. Billy claimed later to know right to the minute when that horse got well, because that was when it cleared that five-barred gate. Mr. Billy said it was exactly five minutes past six in the evening. He and Mrs. Gusto were in that back sitting room of theirs listening to the news on the radio and they had just given the time. He said he was in the act of pulling out his watch to check it when he heard the nickering and snorting. He looked out the window and there was that horse making a circle of the lot, building up speed. Then, he said, it straightened out and sailed over that lot gate with feet to spare and came toward the house, digging every time its feet hit and soaring a good twenty feet to the jump. One of those jumps landed it in the middle of Mrs. Gusto's flower bed, and when it came flying out of there, it flung petunia plants so high that some lodged in the trees around. Mr. Billy said when it went by the house and passed out of his view, it was still picking up speed.

We were sitting on the store porch, Mr. Hayes and I, waiting on Mrs. Theobold to call us to supper. Everyone had left except Cecil Bumpus, and he was just getting in his truck to go, too. We could hear it before we could see it—four quick thuds and a long space, then four more quick thuds and another long space—but we didn't know what it was. We didn't know until it came out of the road that goes to Mr. Billy's and turned on to the one that runs by the store; then for the first second or two, we were still not sure. You see, it had already made up its mind before it reached the intersection where it wanted to go, and when we first saw it, it was leaning so far into the turn its side was almost level with the ground, and we had never seen anything run in that position before, except maybe a motorcycle. It had to swing so wide in the turn because of the speed it was making that when it straightened out it was almost off the road on our side and was lined up on a path that would pass across the store porch and right through where we were sitting. Now we knew what it was, and we were both hollering and trying to get up and to the screen door and inside before disaster struck, knowing all the time it was hopeless. Mr. Hayes did reach the screen door but was blocking his own way, so when he tried to open it, all he managed to do was yank the handle off. Just before it reached the porch, that horse thought better and swerved to go around it. That put it in conflict with Cecil and that pickup. We had forgot about him. I guess when he saw that skyrocket turning the corner he just froze, his truck blocking half the road. There was room to pass behind him, but that horse didn't even try. It took to the air instead, soaring over not the hood or the bed of that truck but the cab, clearing it with room to spare and hitting the ground on the other side already digging again, peppering the side of the truck with gravel like a sawed-off shotgun, and going on down the road, setting off puffs of dust every time it hit, until it passed out of sight around the bend.

Mr. Hayes was still holding that door handle out as if there was a screen door screwed to the end of it. He looked around but couldn't find anything to do with it and finally put it in his pocket.

Cecil stuck his head out the truck window and said, "Where do you reckon he's going to?"

"Not to," Mr. Hayes said, "from. I'd say he's putting distance between him and Billy Gusto, and I guess any other human being unless it would be Odie."

Just then Mrs. Theobold called us to supper, so Cecil went on, and we were trying to get that screen door open without a handle when that Pierce Arrow swung around the corner and slid to a stop. Mr. Billy had enough rope in the back seat to start a business, and he looked as if he meant business, too.

"Did you see it?" he asked. "Which way did it go?"

I started to answer, but Mr. Hayes got in ahead of me. "Are you asking for any reason? I mean, I know you're not planning on tracking it down and trying to put a rope on it and bring it back, because if that was what you had in mind you would have brought Odie with you. And if you was just planning on committing suicide, why you wouldn't go to all the trouble of locating that horse; you would just take some of that rope and hang yourself with it. So I guess you must be asking out of idle curiosity."

Mr. Billy told him to mind his own damn business and started up that Pierce Arrow, but he swung it around and headed back the way he had come, spurting gravel at us.

The next morning Mr. Billy was in Will's truck, because he wouldn't have wanted to take that Pierce Arrow through some of the places he might have to go, with Herman, Will's next to oldest, driving and Will and Odie in the back. They stopped at the store so Odie could tell Big Jack where he had gone and so Mr. Billy could tell Mr. Hayes what I guess he had been thinking about all night.

"I aim to find that horse and then I'm going to put an end to this foolishness," he said and held up a rifle so we could see it. Herman kept looking straight ahead and Will and Odie, riding backwards, kept looking straight behind.

Mr. Hayes said, "You mean you would actually shoot that horse?"

"You just watch me! It's no good to me. I can't even keep it penned up. If a five-barred gate won't hold it, nothing I got will. First thing you know it's going to hurt somebody and then I'll have a lawsuit on my hands."

When they had gone, I said, "I can't understand why Odie would be helping him, or Will or Herman either."

Mr. Hayes rocked back in his chair and looked at me, his mouth turning up just a tiny bit at the corners, which told me that he was way ahead of me. "It wouldn't surprise me," he said, "with all them helping, if he never does find that horse."

He didn't find it either, not that day at least, but he found a lot of people who had seen it, just about everybody who lived along the way. It had left the main road before it got to the river bridge and had taken that dirt track down to Amos Blackburn's place. Amos had a farm down there in the river bottom, which little by little he was clearing of timber. Amos hadn't actually seen it to tell what it was, but sometime in the night he had heard a commotion in his feed lot. He kept four head of horses out there and some milk cows, and he was afraid that a wildcat had come in out of the woods. The fact that no one had ever seen a wildcat anywhere around never stopped the rumors of them or weakened the belief that they existed. When he went out to see about it, he found five horses; however, the next morning, there were only his four. He insisted he couldn't have been mistaken about it, even though it was pitch dark, because he had counted twice to make sure.

So they made a circle of the outside of the lot and found the place where that horse of Mr. Billy's had taken to the air going in and where it had hit coming out. They followed its tracks to the woods where they disappeared. Odie and Will and Herman led Mr. Billy and that rifle around in that woods until they wore him out, but didn't find anything. As they were coming out past the house, Mr. Billy told Amos, "If it shows up again, don't fool with it, it's dangerous. Just come and let me know, and there'll be a five-dollar bill in it for you, providing it's still here when I get here."

The next day, Odie and Herman went back down there and found it, though Herman didn't tell us about that part until later. They left the truck on the main road and made a wide swing around Amos' house to the woods. Herman said Odie went straight to it as if he had known all the time where it was.

He said he had to stay back because that horse wouldn't tolerate him either, but Odie went right up to it and petted it and talked to it and fed it some of the corn they had brought and put some salve on those scratches it had picked up running through the woods.

Odie went back a couple of days later, on his bicycle this time and alone, although he told Herman about it. "He's finding enough to eat," he told Herman, "but he's awful lonesome."

About a week later just before dark, Mr. Hayes and I were on the porch watching a thunderstorm that was on its way when Amos came by. He didn't get out of his truck but spoke to us through the window. "I got it locked in the barn!"

Mr. Hayes brought his chair legs down hard. "You what?"

"That's right. I was setting at the house and saw it sail over that lot fence and right in with the others. And with this storm coming up, when they went into the barn, it went in with them. So I eased out there and shut the door and barred it, and now I'm on my way to tell Mr. Billy."

The minute he left, Mr. Hayes said, "Get the car. We must get Odie."

We overtook Amos before he got to Mr. Billy's and Mr. Hayes said, "Pass him. We don't have that much time."

So I didn't fool around. We boiled the dust on out to the Posers and picked up not only Odie but Will and Herman, too. Amos' truck was still at Mr. Billy's as we passed on our way back. But the rain and dark caught us before we got to Amos' and I had to slow down, so we didn't have a lot of time to spare if Odie was going to get that horse out and back to the woods again before Amos and Mr. Billy got there.

When we came to the turn-off for Amos', I stopped. The

rain was coming in sheets, now. Even with the lightning, you couldn't see much.

Mr. Hayes said, "What's the matter?"

"I'm looking for a place to hide the car."

"No, go on. Odie won't have time to make it on foot. Go on!"

The dirt track was slippery, and I couldn't see half the time, but I drove as fast as I could, splashing and spinning through mud holes and soft spots. Just before we got there, I saw a place I could pull off out of sight but went on to the house. Odie was out of the car and gone before I even got stopped. I wheeled around and went back to the pull-off I had spotted, another dirt track that angled off back into the woods. I had just got in there and the lights off when we saw their lights, and then Amos' truck and that Pierce Arrow went by.

We all jumped from the car and ran through the streaming rain, slipping and sliding and going to our knees in the mud, half blinded by the lightning and deafened by the thunder. As we came around the side of the house, we could see Amos' truck and that Pierce Arrow pulled up to the lot gate and Amos and Mr. Billy getting out, Mr. Billy with that rifle. The lightning was almost constant, now, and the thunder one continuous roll, overtopped at times by louder bangs.

As we got closer, we could see the bar was off the barn door, though it was still shut, so we slowed down, thinking that Odie had made it. Amos and Mr. Billy hadn't noticed anything yet. Amos was opening that lot gate for Mr. Billy when it happened: that barn door flew open and that horse came shooting out of there straight at them.

Mr. Billy's reaction was quick for a man his age. He

slapped that rifle to his shoulder and fired, but his aim was off. The horse stopped, reared up and then wheeled and headed for the fence. Now that we had it in profile, we could see Odie was on its back, bent over and hanging on to its neck.

Maybe Mr. Billy didn't see him. And maybe with all that noise, he didn't hear us hollering. Or maybe, caught up in the swirl and rush of things, he just couldn't stop himself. Anyway, he fired and missed again. And as that horse was gathering itself to clear that fence, he fired the third time, though that one didn't count, because Amos had already hit him and the rifle went off as it flew out of his hands.

The horse leapt. We saw it rise, saw it float to the top of the fence and over and start down. We saw Odie astride it, still leaning forward as if to whisper in its ear. Then came the explosion.

That is what it felt like, an explosion. We were farthest away so we got the least of it and that was bad enough. I found myself on the ground. My head was ringing. Rain was pouring in my face and choking me, but I couldn't feel it yet. All I could feel was pain and tingling, as if I had hit my crazy bone and it had affected my whole body.

Finally, I managed to roll over and get up. Mr. Hayes and Will and Herman were getting up, too, although Mr. Hayes was being slow about it. I went over to help him.

I said, "What happened?" I had to holler through the noise of the rain and thunder and the ringing in my head.

"Lightning!" he said. I couldn't hear him. I had to read his lips. "Struck by lightning!"

We went on then to Amos and Mr. Billy. Amos was all right; that is, he was able to move. Mr. Billy was unconscious. Mr.

Hayes knew what to do, though he wasn't in the best shape to do it. We rolled him over, and Mr. Hayes worked on him until he was breathing again. Then we put him in the back seat of the car and went to look for Odie.

We found him and that horse on the other side of the fence. Dead. Both of them.

We gathered Odie up and took him home, and on the morning of the second day, we buried him. I don't know what happened to the horse. Maybe Amos dragged it off into the woods somewhere.

We all missed Odie, but Will and Herman were especially bereaved. Of all the Posers, they had been the closest. Mr. Hayes said it was because they were all three obsessed and maybe a touch crazy. With Odie, it had been horses. Will was drawn to things beautiful and impractical, like that well-house in his front yard that could have served without apology as a Siamese shrine. Herman had hands that could fashion anything. He would sit talking with you, or rather listening while you talked, shaving away at a piece of wood with his pocket-knife, and before you would know it, he would smile in that timid way he had and hand you a little dog or bird or some other animal, perfectly shaped. Or it might be a head he had made and you would recognize instantly who it was.

A week or so after the funeral, Will and Herman came to the store to see about a stone for Odie's grave. It was the middle of the afternoon and we were alone, Mr. Hayes and I. Will was in no hurry to get to it, so we spent some time remembering Odie. Herman was listening, working on a piece of wood he had brought. After a while, Mr. Hayes reached over and took it from him, turning it over as he looked at it, and then passed it on to me.

It was Odie and that horse as we had last seen them alive, the horse stretched out in the act of leaping and Odie bent forward, his head beside the horse's neck and his mouth open as if speaking. The likeness was unmistakable. But it was not finished. Herman had only roughed out the head and neck of the horse; Odie's head and trunk had not yet been separated from them. I passed it on to Will and watched his face light up.

Mr. Hayes said, "Looks like a centaur, don't it?"

Herman said, "It ain't finished yet." After a bit, he asked, "What's a centaur?"

"Half man, half horse," Mr. Hayes said, and then to me, "Don't you have a picture of one in one of your books?"

I went to my room and brought back an encyclopedia and showed it to Herman. He only glanced at it, then passed it on to Will, who looked and handed it back to me. I took it back to my room, and when I got back, Will had started to talk to Mr. Hayes about the gravestone. Herman was turning that carving over in his hands. He touched Will on the arm and, speaking low, said, "Let's wait on it."

"What?" Will said.

"We don't have to do it today. Let's wait."

They left soon after, but the next day they were back, ready to do business.

"I want a block, six by six by three," Will said.

Mr. Hayes said, "That'll run you some money, Will."

"Wait, I ain't finished. I want another block, six by two by three. How much money we talking about?"

"Why, I don't know. I'll have to inquire."

"If it runs more than I got right now, could you carry me?"

"Yes, I can do that."

"Well, order it then," Will told him.

And Herman said, "Dark, if you can get it."

Mr. Hayes studied Will. Then he studied Herman. Then he said, "Have you got it with you?"

"Got what?" I asked, bothered that I had let him get ahead of me again.

"In the truck," Will said.

Herman went out and brought it back. It was carved out of wood and maybe six inches high, a centaur in the likeness of Odie.

"Do you know how to handle granite?" Mr. Hayes asked Herman.

"I reckon I can learn," Herman said. We didn't doubt him.

They shipped the granite blocks by rail down to Mr. Hayes' sawmill spur. We used one of the flatbed trucks and some mill hands to haul them out and set them in Will's barn. Herman worked on them off and on all winter while Will, and everybody else who could make or take time, watched.

That made the second time that Will had stirred up Zions Cause. The first was when he built that wondrous well-house and dug that dry well. Herman, though he was only fourteen at the time, was in on that, too. They called Will crazy then. Now, they called them both crazy, because they had never heard of a centaur and couldn't get the idea of one straight in their heads.

"You can't tell whether it's a horse in the act of swallering a man or a man in the act of passing a horse," they told one another.

Mrs. Gusto, who as a girl had briefly attended some kind of academy back there in Virginia, where she came from, had other things to say about it. Confusing centaurs with satyrs—

after all, it had been several years since she had been conversant with either—she gave the women lurid accounts of the kind of creatures they were and what their main interest was. "And that's the kind of thing," she said, "that they're proposing to stick up out there among our loved ones."

Her tales were passed on with various embellishments to the husbands. The immediate effect was a heightened interest in Will's barn.

Brother Uriah Thompson, who was then pastor of Zions Cause Church, got in on it, too. That centaur, he concluded, constituted a graven image and such was explicitly prohibited by the Scriptures. Moreover, it was not even a Christian representation but a heathen one.

Mrs. Blackburn took direction from both of them, and before Herman had put the finishing touches to his work, she was out engaged in a house-to-house campaign to gain support for a resolution the three of them had drafted to be put before the congregation of Zions Cause Church forbidding the erection in the church graveyard of any statue, figure or graven image or any other form or representation not of a Christian theme or nature.

"Can they do that?" Will asked. He and Herman were getting concerned and had come to see Mr. Hayes about it.

"Well, Mrs. Gusto is much looked up to. And Brother Uriah will automatically carry a good number along with him. And Mrs. Blackburn has worried everybody so much that some will vote for it just to get a little peace and quiet. Yes, I think they stand a good chance of getting the church to go along with them."

"Then what can be done?"

"I'd say three things. One, you can just put that centaur out in your front yard and let it go at that. Now wait a minute! I know you're not going to be satisfied with that. Two, you can move Odie onto your own land where can't nobody tell you what you can or cannot do. Yes, I can see that don't suit you either."

Herman said softly, "You said three things."

"That's right," said Mr. Hayes. "The third thing is something I can do and what I'm prepared to do come Wednesday night when they hold that business meeting at the church."

When Mr. Hayes and I got there that night, the rear two-thirds of the church was already pretty much filled, so we sat down close to the front. By the time the meeting started, they had just about filled it all. All the Posers were there, Will and Herman sitting together next to the aisle, then Bessie and the others. Across the aisle from us was Mrs. Blackburn, with Rile on one side and Amos on the other. Mr. Billy and Mrs. Gusto were among the last, and they sat in front of the Blackburns.

The pulpit of the church was raised two steps above the level of the sanctuary and was enclosed by a low rail. Brother Uriah, who was an enthusiastic preacher, had been known in the heat of a sermon to leap over that rail and land hard in the sanctuary to emphasize a point. He was sitting there in a chair behind the pulpit. When everyone was settled, he stood up and started the meeting, going through the opening prayer and other preliminaries and finally getting to it.

"Beloved of the Lord," he said, "we have a serious matter before us tonight. It concerns a statue, a graven image, if you will, that's about to be erected out yonder in the church burying ground. Now, I read in my Bible where it says not to do that. Make no graven image, the Lord tells us. Now, you can't speak plainer than that. Furthermore, this image we're talking about is ungodly. It's unnatural. It's unchristian. Yes, it's a heathen image! An abomination in the sight of the Lord! Now, that's what they want to set up out yonder in our graveyard.

"Now, we all knew and loved little Odie. And we know and love Brother Will and young Brother Herman there. We share their grief. But they may not know what they're about to do. So we owe it to them. Yes, because we love them, we owe it to them, I say, to help them not to do this thing."

I could see Rile and Amos. They were both looking at the floor. I couldn't see Will and Herman without turning around, and I didn't want to do that.

"Now, I have here a resolution. I helped on it, but the real work was done by two of our good sisters in the Lord, Mrs. Gusto and Mrs. Blackburn. They can't say anything because the Scripture says that women are to keep silent in the church, but I want them to have the credit."

They were taking it, too, both sitting up straight as Brother Uriah read the resolution.

"All right," Brother Uriah said when he had finished, "do I hear a motion on this matter?"

Mrs. Gusto nudged Mr. Billy to his feet.

"I so move that we adopt the resolution."

Somebody seconded, and Brother Uriah said, "Are we ready for the question?"

Mr. Hayes rose and said, "If I might say just a word."

Brother Uriah hadn't expected it, and he didn't look pleased. "Brother Hayes, are you a member of this church?" he asked, knowing full well he wasn't. Mr. Hayes was a religious man in his own way, which was different from theirs, and besides, he had other reasons for not joining.

Mr. Hayes said, "I believe what I have to say has a bearing on the question before you."

It had got to be too much for Rile. Before Mrs. Blackburn could stop him, he stood up and said, "Preacher, I think we ought to listen to Mr. Hayes."

There were several agreements. Brother Uriah looked even less pleased, but he motioned Mr. Hayes to go ahead.

Mr. Hayes turned around and spoke to the crowd.

"You all know how this church come to be built. You also know why it was built here. Now, the graveyard is a mile or more out the Gusto Road. It was there before the church, has been there maybe a hundred years, long before my time, anyway. What you may not know is that I own across the road from Mr. Billy Gusto, on the side where the graveyard is. I bought it from Mrs. Theobold soon after Ish died. Mrs. Theobold's boy still farms it, but the land belongs to me."

I looked at Brother Uriah and Mrs. Gusto and Mrs. Blackburn. None of them saw it coming.

"Well, the other day I got to looking at my deed. It says nothing about the graveyard."

They still didn't see it. He had to tell them.

"What I'm saying is, the deed don't carry my property line around the graveyard, it *includes* it. That graveyard is mine."

They saw that much now, and maybe they were beginning to see the rest of it. Mrs. Blackburn was huffing between Rile and Amos, and Mrs. Gusto was hissing to Mr. Billy. Brother

Uriah was red in the face. He said, "You can't own a grave-yard, not where other folks are buried. There's a law!"

Mr. Hayes said, "I've taken legal advice on that. What the law says is that I can't destroy it. It don't say I've got to maintain it and it don't say I've got to let anybody else be buried there. I can't go in and knock over the gravestones and plow it up. But otherwise it's mine to do with as I see fit."

That shocked them all. They sat in deep silence.

"Now, I want to be reasonable about it," Mr. Hayes said. "I don't feel I ought to own that graveyard, even though the law says it's mine. So I've had a deed of gift drawn up which assigns it to the church." He held it up for everybody to see. "But wait, now, there's a condition. The condition is, and it's spelled out in the deed, that anybody can put up any kind of marker or monument that suits them."

Mr. Billy, who valued land more than most, didn't take time to think but by reflex popped to his feet. Mrs. Gusto, who must have known what he was about to do because she had lived with him too long not to, yanked at his shirt sleeve trying to pull him down, but he ignored her and said, "Brother Uriah, I move you that we accept Jim Hayes' deed of gift."

By the reaction of the crowd, Brother Uriah could tell that he had been beat but wouldn't accept it. "I believe there's already a motion on the floor," he said.

"I made it and I withdraw it in favor of this one," Mr. Billy said.

Brother Uriah still would not give up. "The second will have to be withdrawn, too."

It was. And with the vote on Mr. Billy's motion, Zions Cause

Church had what everybody thought it had all along, a grave-yard of its own.

The erection of the centaur drew a big crowd. It amounted to a memorial celebration for Odie. We used one of the saw-mill trucks. We didn't need the mill hands because we had so many volunteers. The smaller of those two blocks of granite they used for the base stone. Herman had set four pins in it which would slip into the holes he had made in each hoof of the centaur and anchor it. On the side next to the grave he had carved

O. D. Poser
Born July 12, 1921
Died September 29, 1935

It was the first time any of us had seen his name written or knew that it was actually O. D. and not Odie as we had always called him.

When we manhandled the centaur onto the base stone, there were too many of us wanting to help, to have a part in it, at least to be touching it as it went down over those pins. As it settled into place, there was a cheer from the crowd. Then we stepped back and looked and were silent for a while until somebody said, "Amen!" And then we all laughed and slapped each other on the back and milled around Will and Herman and slapped them on the back, too.

As Mr. Hayes and I were leaving, Amos walked out with us. When we reached the road, we turned for a last look at the centaur. It was a perfect likeness. Herman had never done better. And if he could ever have envisioned it, it was exactly what Odie would have wanted.

As we turned away, Amos said, "You know, he never has paid me that five dollars he promised."

"What?" Mr. Hayes said.

"Mr. Billy. He promised me five dollars for letting him know about that horse, and he never has paid me. I hate to have to ask him for it. A man ought not have to be asked."

Beloved Sarah
[1938]

"I want to talk to you about your soul," she told me. I had
brought her to the living quarters behind the store, to the sitting room. It was, I suppose, the first time she had been there.

Her name was Sarah. She was wife to Uriah Thompson,
pastor of Zions Cause Church. Following custom, everyone
called him Brother Uriah and her Sister Sarah. Four years before at the invitation of Brother Jesse Jordon, who then was
pastor, Brother Uriah had served as visiting evangelist for the
spring revival meeting at the church, and everyone had liked
him so well that when a year later Brother Jesse left, they
called Brother Uriah to take his place.

She was tall for a woman and slender and much younger
than Brother Uriah. She was in fact twenty-eight, while he
must have been forty-five or fifty, but the joke that was bound
to be made about that was short-lived because they soon
gained widespread respect, each in his own way. Where there
was trouble, they would be there: Brother Uriah first with
prayer and stern counsel and sometimes forthright condemna-

tion; Sister Sarah following later with comfort and sympathy and whatever was needed in the way of nursing and cooking and cleaning. It was said of Brother Uriah that he was a man of the Lord and could make you smell brimstone; of Sister Sarah that she was a good Christian woman and a comfort and stay in time of trouble.

I knew her to speak to—she was in the store from time to time—but not to talk to. So I was a little puzzled that after-noon when she came and asked for a word with me in private. But Mr. Hayes, at his desk in the back of the store from which he conducted his now considerable business affairs, looked at the small white Bible she was carrying and raised a knowing eyebrow to me as we passed on our way to the living quarters.

She had taken more time than she needed getting to it, showing instead an interest in the room and its furnishings, especially the sword and matched pistols over the mantel, which Mr. Hayes had brought back from the Spanish-American War. At last, after a deep breath, she told me she had come about my soul.

I had not expected it, but I was not really surprised either. I was eighteen years old and still not a born-again Christian, and in Zions Cause it was generally and strongly believed that if you had not been born again, you were utterly lost and con-demned to everlasting torment. It was understandable, then, that the saved in the community would be concerned over the lost. That concern became strongest during the spring revival, an annual event with an evangelist brought in to conduct a week-long series of meetings. The first part of the week was devoted to renewing the faith and dedication of the congrega-tion, the saved. The remainder was given over to winning lost souls to Christ and bringing them into the church. It was during this time that those few in the community who had reached the age of accountability, somewhere around twelve years old, but who had not experienced rebirth could count on being visited and exhorted to salvation. But this year's revival had ended over a month ago, so I had not really expected to be set upon again so soon.

It was not that I resisted rebirth. Considering the rich reward involved and the enormity of the penalty for rejection, anyone would have had to be an outright fool not to snatch it, given the opportunity. But to qualify required evidently a belief much stronger than I could muster, and in my case at least, belief was not an act of choice. I could no more will to believe that I could will not to believe.

As a matter of fact, I believed just enough to be uneasy about the hereafter, the Gates of Hell and beyond having been represented to me in graphic detail, and I would have welcomed being totally convinced. But I soon saw that she was not going to be able to do it, not the way she was going about it.

She was using the same old arguments, the same stock phrases and assertions and scriptural quotations that I had heard a hundred times before, reeling them off as if by rote. I thought how presumptuous it was of her, this good Christian woman, to put me through this without any assurance or even hope of success; and how audacious, because if she had bothered to think about it at all, she would have known that there would have been several ahead of her with at least as much as she was offering who had failed; and what a low esteem she must have of me as a competent human being to think that I would not have myself, long since and without having to be urged to it by anyone, carefully considered and weighed what she was giving me and more besides.

My face must have reflected my thoughts. And too, as I learned later, she had been aware of the futility of what she was doing from the first and was finally convinced of it. She stopped, cut off in midsentence, bit her lip and closed her eyes. I waited, uncertain whether she would pray or cry. She did neither. After a while, she looked at me again and said softly, "I'm sorry," and began to gather her things up to go.

She got as far as the door before she turned and said, "No, wait. It was foolish of me to think that it would be simple, that this is all it would take. Give me some time. An afternoon a week for a while. Is that possible?"

It was possible. Mr. Hayes could mind the store, and if he was busy, we could always call on Mrs. Theobold. I didn't think much of the idea, but I wouldn't lie to her.

"Will you do it, then, give me the time?" She touched my arm and looked up at me, concern creasing her forehead and drawing worry lines between her brows. I felt sure if I said no, she would have accepted it. I wanted to but heard myself saying yes instead.

"Good," she said, smiling now. "Good! I'll come back tomorrow, if that's all right."

"That didn't take long," Mr. Hayes said when she had gone. "You must not be as hardened a case as everyone thought."

"She's not through," I said. "I've just committed one of your afternoons a week to minding the store while she works on me some more."

"If you can stand it," he said, "I reckon I can."

"I'm not any good at it," she said the next day. " You would think after all this time I would have learned how to lead souls to Christ, but somehow I haven't." We were at the graveyard. She was sitting on the base stone of the centaur that marked Odie Poser's grave, leaning back to look up at me as she explained.

"Everyone thought it was such a good idea, and I did, too, at first. We were looking for something we could do, the women of the church, some project, some goal we could strive for; and we decided to make a special effort with those who had not come forward during the revival, the older ones in particular, lest they become hardened through repeatedly turning away. So we made a list. And then someone said that each of us should pick a name and be totally responsible for just that one. But two or three wanted the same person, and there were others on the list that nobody chose. Then someone else, Mrs. Blackburn, I think, said let the Lord decide; so she put the names in the collection plate and had each of us draw one. I waited and took the last one. It was you."

When I had come to the store porch that afternoon to watch for her, she was already there, waiting at the foot of the steps, the small white Bible sticking out of the pocket of her skirt. She had said, "Why don't we walk?"

It was early May, and the sun was warm. I was glad not to have to spend the afternoon inside. At the corner she turned down the Gusto road, and we had come all the way to the graveyard before she stopped.

"They told me I'd have my work cut out for me," she said, smiling to soften what would have seemed to her criticism. "They said you read too much and your head was full of notions and that Mr. Hayes didn't help either. So it wasn't that I was not warned. It was just that I didn't know what else to do. And then in the middle of it, I knew it wasn't working and I couldn't go on. I wanted to give up, had decided to in fact, but then realized I couldn't. I thought maybe with enough time I could find a way."

All the way to the graveyard, I had kept waiting for her to start on me, but she had just made polite conversation as if we were two people who just happened to be taking the same road and were walking along together. We came past the Gusto place and the lane that goes back to the Posers and on to the graveyard where she turned in. She sat down on the base stone of the centaur and lifted her face to the sun. I followed and stood with an arm braced against the centaur as she explained.

"So I asked for an afternoon a week. That may not be enough, I know, but it was all I dared ask for, and even then I was afraid you'd say no."

"I thought about it," I said. "I wanted to."

"But you didn't, and that's a good sign."

"How will you go about it?" I asked.

"I don't know. I thought maybe if I got to know you better it would help. And maybe God will show me a way. After all, He arranged it. He must have had a reason."

I thought blind chance was a better explanation but didn't say so.

"Maybe you can tell me what I ought to do," she said.

If I knew that, I thought, there would be no reason for us to be here.

She didn't seem to expect me to answer. She stood up and began to circle the statue, walking like a man, thumbs hooked into the pockets of her skirt, taking overlong strides, her whole body pivoting with each step. The act somehow accentuated her femininity. She completed the circle, stopped and studied the centaur, the upper portion a portrayal of Odie.

"It's a good likeness. I'm glad they were allowed to put it up."

No thanks to Brother Uriah, I thought, and Mrs. Gusto and Mrs. Blackburn.

"Uriah was so set against it, and I suppose it is unchristian, but I really couldn't see the harm."

My face must have given me away for she spoke in his defense.

"He did what he thought was right, and Mrs. Gusto and Mrs. Blackburn, too."

I said, "If you're going to interfere, you have a responsibility to be right."

"Yes, that's true. But it's not always easy, especially when you're faced with two rights that contradict each other." She seemed to be speaking more to herself than to me, but I felt properly answered.

She came and sat down again on the base stone. "You were there when it happened." She was speaking now of Odie being struck by lightning. "Tell me about it."

She would already have known, of course, but maybe not an eyewitness account—there were only six of us who saw it— and then, too, she and Brother Uriah had not been in Zions Cause long when it happened, so I told it all, just as I had seen it.

"It didn't actually strike them directly, we learned later. It hit a tree a few yards away and I guess was branching along the ground when that horse touched down. Hair was burned on one foreleg, and Odie's shoe on that side was missing. They found it the next day some distance away. It must have killed them both instantly."

She reached out and touched the back of my hand with her fingertips. "Hearing you tell it is like being there. I can almost see it."

The telling had put a spell on both of us. After a while, she broke it to say, "It could just as well have been you. Have you ever wondered why you were spared?"

"I was too far away from the strike," I said, and then I realized that she had asked a different question. "No, I don't know why."

"I'm convinced there is a reason." Then a smile softened her seriousness. She stood up and touched my arm again. "Someday we will find out what it is."

I noticed that she had said "we" and wondered if she was aware of it.

Maybe she was still pursuing the subject when she asked, "What will you do now that you are out of school? Will you go on to college?"

"Not right away."

"Why not?"

"There's no rush. Besides, I haven't made up my mind what I want to do."

"What have you thought about?"

"The law. I've thought about becoming a lawyer. I know that would please Mr. Hayes, but he will want me to make up my own mind. Whatever I turn out to be, I want it to be here."

"Because of the people," she said. "You see all their faults, but you still feel a great tenderness for them. I believe you even feel a responsibility for them." Then she smiled at me. "You see, I know that much about you already."

"How could you possibly know that, even if it was true?"

"You told me," she said, "when you told me the story of Odie."

I said, "There are some I would have a hard time feeling tender toward. Anyway, it's not only the people. It's the land, too."

I was suddenly aware that I felt at ease with her, trusted her, that she had a gentleness that made it unnecessary for me to be guarded, and that I was telling her things I had never spoken to anyone before, not even to Mr. Hayes.

We talked on, I doing most of it, and the afternoon slipped away. I was sorry when it was time to go.

When we reached the store, she said, "Same time, next week, if that's all right with you."

It was. It also turned out to be a long week.

When it was finally over, we went back to the graveyard. As we turned in, she took my arm and said, "Show me around."

So we took the tour. She wanted to know each one's story. Most of them I knew, if not first-hand then at second or third. After all, I had spent my life at the store, listening.

"You are able to bring them to life," she said. "You make me see them. That's a gift."

"I've had good teachers, just about everybody in Zions Cause at one time or another. Sooner or later it all gets hashed over at the store, usually several versions. I just choose what seems best and fill in the rest."

We came at last to our lot, Mr. Hayes' and mine, with the identical graves except for the inscriptions on the stones.

"Amanda Hayes," she read.

"Mr. Hayes' wife and my aunt. She died of tuberculosis a few years before I was born. By all accounts, a complaining woman whose life turned out just the way she thought it would."

"And Susan Wells?" she asked, reading the other inscription.

"My mother. Surely you must have heard the story."

"I've heard bit and pieces, mostly contradictory."

"A lot of it is speculation, has to be. Mr. Hayes, and he's the only person who would know the whole of it, refuses to talk about it."

"They said she was . . . different," she said.

"No," I corrected her, "they would have said she was peculiar. It was a mental problem. She was withdrawn to the point of not really living in the same world as other people. She was able to rouse herself just enough to cope with routine, enough in any event to look after Mrs. Hayes in the last stages."

"But she stayed on after Mrs. Hayes died."

"She had no other place to go. Besides, he loved her and would not have let her go."

"But he didn't marry her."

"How could he? For him at least that would have taken the involvement of both of them, and he could never penetrate to where she was or call her forth to him. And through bitter experience, he would have known that a marriage of any other kind is no marriage at all. Worse, maybe."

"Yes, I can see that," she said. "So he resigned himself."

"Until that preacher came through. There was no church here then. They built a brush arbor next to the store where he preached and performed the healing miracles. And witnessing them, Mr. Hayes was seized with the wild hope that he could cure Susan. So he took him to her and left them alone through the night. The next morning, the preacher had disappeared, and Susan was the same. Well, not quite the same, but they didn't find that out until later. They had already built Zions Cause Church in commemoration of the healing miracles when it became obvious to everyone that Susan was going to have a child. She died giving birth to me, or a few days later."

"And the preacher, your father?"

"Only by blood. Never heard of again. No one ever knew where he came from or where he went to."

"Is that why . . . ?"

"No, I don't think so. I don't feel about him one way or another. From what I've been able to find out, he was not whole either. I don't blame him or what he represented. If it has affected my attitude toward religion, I'm not aware of it."

"So you lived with Mr. Hayes?" she said.

"There were others who would have taken me, but he claimed me. Maybe in the beginning because I was at least half Susan's, although they say I look like him, that preacher. I never became a son to Mr. Hayes, nor he a father to me. What we are to each other is something different and I think stronger than that."

She had been looking at the gravestones as we talked. She turned to me then and reached up and took my face between her hands and held it for a long moment. Her touch was soft, but even after she had taken her hands away, I could still feel their pressure.

"I guess we should go now," she said.

When she left me at the store, she said she would see me the same afternoon of the next week. It didn't work out. Mr. Hayes came back from making his rounds that morning with the news that the day before old Mrs. Goins, who was in her seventies and lived alone, had fallen and broken her hip. He had gone by to see what he could do and had found Sarah there. She had been there all night and would be staying through Saturday when Mrs. Goins' married daughter who lived in St. Louis could get free and come and take over.

"She said tell you she wouldn't be able to see you at all this week," he said, "and she asked me to give you this." He handed me a folded note.

It said: "Come to church Sunday. Please."

I wadded it up and jammed it in my pocket.

Mr. Hayes said, "You don't seem too pleased at getting off the hook."

"I'll manage to struggle through," I said, but I hadn't fooled him. And he was right, I wasn't pleased. In fact, I was outright disappointed and inclined to be childish about it. Surely she could have found somebody to spell her for an afternoon. Wasn't a soul a sight more important than a broken hip? She not only didn't know how to go about things, she couldn't even get her priorities straight.

"If I ever get down and you can't manage," Mr. Hayes said, "I want you to send for her."

"Why do you say that?"

"Because I know she would be doing it for the same reason you would."

It took me some time to figure out what he was talking about, and then I wondered if he had been reading my mind and was speaking to my innermost thoughts.

On Sunday I went to church. As I was getting ready, Mr. Hayes was careful not to remark on it, which was somehow worse than if he had. Unlike him, I had attended Sunday services before. When I was younger, I had gone quite regularly to Sunday School and church, too, taken by Mrs. Theobold. But it had been several years now since I had attended a service, except for funerals; we both went to them.

"I just feel like it," I told Mr. Hayes as I was leaving.

"Then, by all means, do it," he said.

I would have liked to have sat in the back, but I didn't get there in time—the church always filled up from the rear forward—so I had to pass most of the congregation on my way to the front. It stirred up some whispers.

There was a section at the front extending about two-thirds the width of the church that was raised two steps above the level of the sanctuary. The pulpit was located there and a small choir. The choir was just standing to sing as I sat down. Sarah was there in the first row. She didn't look at me until the hymn was finished and they were seated again. Then she caught my eye and said, "Thank you," mouthing the words to me, but most everyone could read her lips as well as I, and those who couldn't asked their neighbors, so that from all over the church I could hear them whispering, "She told him thank you." It was a little embarrassing but not unexpected. Everything that happened in Zions Cause was automatically everybody's business, so I was sure it was general if not universal knowledge that I was her personal responsibility, assigned so by divine intent when she drew my name out of that collection plate, and they were naturally interested in any progress she was making.

I had heard Brother Uriah preach at funerals, so I knew what to expect, an emotional sermon, rhythmic, even at times poetic, with a lot of shouting but not much substance, effective, however, in that it created a mood appropriate to the point of it all, which was the invitation to salvation that came at the end.

The invitation was ritualistic. The simple and sketchy instructions were given and repeated throughout: *Believe in Christ, trust in Jesus, for whosoever believeth in Him and is baptized hath everlasting life.* Then the invitation hymn, slow and pleading: *Just as I am, without one plea, but that Thy blood was shed for me, and that Thou bidst me come to Thee; Oh Lamb of God, I come . . . I come.* And the prayer, with choir and congregation singing softly in the background: *Oh Lord, we feel in our hearts there is someone out there who is troubled, someone who is longing for salvation, someone who is almost at the point of acceptance. And, Lord, you know this may be their last opportunity. Life is so uncertain. They may walk out of here today and step right into eternal and everlasting torment. But, Lord, they are almost ready to accept You as their savior. So close, so close. Lord, let them come.*

At this point the ritual may be varied. Sometimes individual members of the congregation may be moved to go to a lost soul and take him by the hand and plead with him to accept salvation, while the rest of the congregation looks on and the preacher offers encouragement from the pulpit.

This was the possibility I was dreading: that now they had

me in church, and I had come willingly and without con-
ditions, the several who had exhorted me through the years
would feel moved to renew their efforts. But I need not have
worried. They were leaving it up to her. I was now her responsibility, and she would judge when the time was right. And
she was singing, not even looking at me. And so the invitation
ended, and Brother Uriah called on someone to give the benediction and made his way to the door to be ready to shake
hands with them all as they left.

Several made it a point to speak to me and say they were
glad to see me, so it took awhile for me to make my way to the
door. Brother Uriah shook my hand and slapped me on the
shoulder and told me he was praying for me. Sarah was in
the churchyard smiling at me over Mrs. Blackburn's shoulder.
As I came up to them, Mrs. Blackburn was saying, "Well,
you've already done more than anybody else has, you got him
to church."

Mrs. Blackburn, misjudging Sarah's laugh, went on without
ever knowing I was there. Sarah took my hand and held it and
said, "You've made me very happy. Thank you."

I said, "When will I see you?"

"Tomorrow, if you will be free. And if the weather is all
right, maybe you will show me where Ish Theobold found that
big fish."

The weather was beautiful, and Sarah was a match for it.
She was wearing a print dress, white with tiny blue flowers,
with a fitted bodice and flared skirt. Her hair, usually done up
in a tight bun, was pulled back and caught by a clasp and fell
almost to her waist. She was carrying her little white Bible.
Mr. Hayes was in his chair on the store porch, and as they

spoke to each other, I sensed a warmth between them that I had not noticed before, not an intimacy but something of a mutual respect. He looked at her dress and said we had better take a blanket to sit on, so I went back and got one. He saw us off with that faint smile of his which always told me that he knew something I didn't.

We went on past the graveyard and left the road and, skirting the cornfield that Will, Ish and Mrs. Theobold's son, had already planted, came at last to the bend in the creek where long ago Ish had battled and been bested by a fish almost as big as he was. I had told her the story before at the graveyard.

I spread the blanket on a patch of grass. She left her Bible there, and we walked to the water's edge. The pool was almost clear. The green scum which covered it in summer had not yet started to grow.

"You saw it happen?" she asked.

"Yes, most of it. Not when he drowned. He was alone then. Will found him."

"But it was so long ago. You couldn't have been very old."

"I was five. And I have a good memory."

"And now you are what, eighteen?"

"Yes."

"I married the year I was eighteen, but you are much older than I was then." And then after a pause, she added, "Now I'm twenty-eight. And I am beginning to doubt if I have caught up with you yet."

"How did you come to marry him?" I asked.

"Oh, Uriah was a friend of the family, especially of my father. When I was a very little girl, he came to pastor our church. He was in his early twenties then and single, and he lived with us for a while. My father was only a few years older, and they became very close. After a year or two Uriah married and found a house of his own. Eventually he accepted the call of another church and moved there, but they still kept in touch, and he and his wife would visit us occasionally. Uriah was different then. He was always laughing and joking, and from the time I was a child, he had enjoyed teasing me. His wife Mary was very pretty and very kind and we all loved her. They were especially close and their happiness seemed to spill over to everyone around them."

"What happened to her?"

"She died of cancer. Not an easy death. Uriah personally nursed her to the end. It was as if part of him, the happiness, died with her."

She turned away and went to the blanket and sat down, taking a long time adjusting her dress. I followed and sat facing her. After a while she went on.

"After Mary died, Uriah used to visit us often. He needed my father. He couldn't accept it. My father helped him to reconcile himself to it, but he was never the same. After a while, my father began encouraging Uriah to marry again, telling him a pastor needed a wife to help him in his work. I was growing up then, and my father got it in his mind that the two of us should marry."

The thought that she would settle for so little just to please her father sparked a blind anger in me. I could hear it in my voice when I asked, "And that was it? You just got married?"

"No," she said, laughing to soothe me, "of course not. He had to put the idea in our minds and we had to get used to it. That took some time. Uriah was really the only man I had ever known. Oh, I had known boys in school, boys my own age, but my father never allowed me to go out with any of them. He wouldn't even let them come to see me at home. He had very strict ideas about that, and then too, I was his only child. After a while, they stopped asking. My last year in school, Uriah began to invite me to go with him to church affairs. My father agreed to that, maybe even encouraged him to do it. Then soon after I graduated, Uriah asked me to marry him. When I discussed it with my father, he said it was something he had prayed for for a long time. Uriah had always seemed like a brother to me, and he was a very dear friend. I wanted to help him and to do the kind of work I would do as his wife, God's work. So we married."

"You haven't said anything about love."

"No, but there are different kinds of love."

"Oh, sure." I was furious with her. "There is love for fathers and love for brothers and love for friends . . ."

"And love for God," she said softly.

But I was beyond control now and would not be stopped. "And love between a man and woman"—I was shouting—"like the love between Uriah and his first wife!"

In the silence that followed she looked at me, stricken, and then she began to cry. I found that I was crying, too. Then without thought, we reached for each other.

There is a belief held by some that the world is not given, that it is rather the creation, the construction of our senses, thought and will. If so, our world changed, contracted, its four corners coinciding with those of the blanket on which we lay, and existed without past or future. Certainly nothing more registered upon our awareness. We spent the rest of the afternoon holding hands and looking into each other's eyes and speaking when at all only in the language of lovers.

Finally, we knew that we must go. We got up. I folded the blanket. And then she remembered the Bible she had brought. We found it at the edge of the grass where it had fallen. She picked it up and noticed a stain on one corner of the cover where it had lain on a damp spot of earth. She scrubbed at it with her handkerchief and then smiled and said, "It doesn't matter. I'll wash it off when I get home."

We were mostly silent on the way home, experiencing a sense of oneness that was new to both of us. When we parted at the store, there was no need to make arrangements about seeing each other again. We both understood that we would meet the next afternoon. The feeling went on after she was gone. It was still there the next morning when she came hurrying into the store to tell me that she had been sent for again and would not be able to meet with me.

"I'll come with you," I said.

"No! You mustn't."

"But when will I see you?"

"I don't know. I'll come as soon as I'm free. I must go now. Uriah is waiting in the car."

It was three days before we got together again. Mrs. Goins' daughter had been called back to St. Louis by some crisis in her own family. It took that long for a permanent replacement to be found.

By unspoken agreement we didn't go to the graveyard or to the creek; we went to the church and sat on the steps. She was carrying her Bible and put it down on the step beside her. The yellow stain on the corner was almost imperceptible. Maybe it was not there at all except in my imagination.

"I don't understand," she said. "He arranged it. He must have known what would happen. Why would He do it, then?"

"Maybe this is what He meant to happen," I said, assuming her hypothesis.

"But surely not!"

"Why not? Does it seem so wrong to you?"

"No!" she said. "No! Just the opposite. I've never felt anything to be so right. But feeling so doesn't make it so. And others would think it was wrong."

"Yes, it would be wrong to them. But then, we don't have to let them know."

We sat in silence for a while, and then she said, "When did you know?"

"At the creek, when you were telling me about your marriage. I realized that I loved you in a way Uriah never would, and the unfairness made me furious."

"Then I knew before you. At the graveyard when you talked about the relationship between you and Mr. Hayes, I knew then that I loved you as I had never loved before. And when you came to church because I asked you, I felt you were beginning to love me." After a pause, she added, "I'm glad. If there is punishment, and there will be, it will fall heaviest on me because I am the most guilty."

"Why you?" I asked. "Could you have done anything about it? Did you have the power to stop it?"

"No, I'm sure I couldn't. But even if I could, I don't think I would have. So you see, that doesn't absolve me."

We explored the questions of sin and guilt and divine intent the rest of the afternoon but found no answers. After that, I never remember our discussing such things again. As we were parting, she said, "I guess the only thing to do is see to it that we don't hurt anyone and then take what comes."

We continued to spend time together on more or less a regular basis all that summer. I was in church every Sunday because it pleased Sarah to see me there. And she would openly smile her pleasure to me from the choir. The congregation was deceived. They congratulated her on getting me there. And if I continued to resist salvation, well, it was known that I was a hard case, and at least she had got me to take the first step. It disturbed Sarah to deceive them, but there was nothing we could do about it. And she would not accept my argument that really they were deceiving themselves.

Over the course of the summer, we covered the whole Zions Cause area. When the weather was bad, we would go to the store or the parsonage. At the store, we would invite Mr. Hayes to join us, and a strong friendship sprang up between him and Sarah. At the parsonage, Uriah would sometimes sit with us. Though we never became friends, I did become easy with him. I never felt I had taken anything from him.

Although we went back there at times, what happened at the creek never happened again. If it had, we would not have regretted it any more than we had the first time. It just didn't happen. Oh, we touched sometimes, and embraced and kissed, when we were alone and felt the need to, but as time went on that grew less. The sense of oneness, however, never diminished.

Toward the end of August, Sarah came to the store one afternoon and asked to speak to me in private. I called Mrs. Theobold out, and we went back to the sitting room. She told me quickly: Uriah had been called to pastor another church and he felt he should accept the offer.

"Where?" I asked.

"Mayfield."

"But that's seventy-five miles away!"

"I know."

"When?"

"Next month." She sat down on the couch, looking as desolate as I felt.

"So this is the punishment," she said.

"Talk him out of it," I said. "Refuse to go."

"No. We agreed we would take whatever came."

At least, she had, and I would not ask her to go back on her bargain with God. I sat beside her, and we held hands, sharing the misery. We were still that way when Mr. Hayes came in. He looked at us and asked what had happened.

"They're moving," I told him.

"Oh," he said and looked relieved. "Well, maybe it's for the best."

"What do you mean, for the best!"

He gave it to us, then, softening it with a smile for Sarah, which he wouldn't have done for me.

"Just how long do you two reckon you can keep that bunch fooled? Do you think it can go on forever!"

"You know?" we asked.

"How could I not know! You surely didn't think that because everybody else has been walking around with their eyes shut, I would join them just for the company."

"But you didn't say anything," we said.

"There was no need. But I would have had to soon for your own protection."

"You mean you approve?"

"Yes. I know a little something about loving."

And there it was: the first time that I had ever heard him, however obliquely, refer to Susan.

But something was bothering me and I had to ask. "Why did you look so relieved when we told you they were leaving?"

He turned to Sarah. "I thought it might have been something else."

"That I was pregnant," she said.

"It has been known to follow."

"To follow!" I said. "So you knew that, too. And probably when." Then I remembered it was he who had made me take the blanket. "He even knew before!" I told Sarah.

"It was a pretty day and a pretty girl and you were in love even if you didn't know it yet. It was going to happen sometime. I didn't see any sense in that pretty dress getting messed up."

"Is there anything you don't know?" Sarah asked.

"I don't know how either one of us is going to get along without you," he said in all seriousness.

She went to him and put her arms around him and kissed him. "I love you, too," she told him.

In the days we had left, we reconciled ourselves. It helped that Mr. Hayes had made us realize that we would have had to give it up soon anyway or come out in the open, which we would not have done. At the last, Sarah said, "If you ever need me, send for me and I'll come."

"And what about Uriah?" I asked.

"If you send, I will know you need me more than Uriah."

She asked me to write her at least once a week and tell her all that had happened. "It will be like being here," she said. "You could always make me see things."

I wrote regularly, and she did, too. Early on, I fell into the habit, which continued, of beginning my letters to her, "Beloved Sarah." Several times over the next few years, Mr. Hayes and I drove there to visit. Then came the war and I enlisted and was sent overseas. Her letters and her love sustained me through all those years and beyond. We never lost the sense of oneness.

The Graveyard
[1940]

The graveyard was the last to go. The houses and barns had all
been razed, the lumber worth saving hauled off to what was
already being called New Zion, and the rest burned. Where
there had been chimneys and foundations, these had been
knocked down and scattered. What timber there was had been
cut, the good logs passing through Mr. Hayes' sawmill on their
way to New Zion, the trash left lying where it fell so that one
day it would snag and hold forever prized and expensive fish-
ing lures of vacationers. The whole area lay devastated await-
ing the deluge which would follow the closing of the gates of
the now completed TVA dam creating the largest man-made
lake in the world. Only the graveyard remained, and it would
have to go, too.

By design, the graveyard would have adjoined the church,
which was located more than a mile away and well above
where the waterline would be. But the graveyard predated the
church, which had to be built where it was because that was
where nearly twenty years before the healing miracles took

place and the church was built to commemorate them. Now the graveyard was going where design would have put it in the first place, to a plot back of Zions Cause Church. As it would turn out, that was going to be wrong, too, because within two years Zions Cause Church would be abandoned for a new church in New Zion, where most of them would live, and the new site for the graveyard would then be more than twice as far from the church as the old one.

Anyway, come Hell or high water, the latter at least certain, the graveyard was going to be moved. The new site was all ready: purchased and prepared at the expense of the federal government, the family plots chosen or assigned and the new graves dug and waiting. The next of kin, or the closest they could come to it, had been sent official notices telling them the time and ordering them to be there to witness the move and afterward to sign a statement that it had been done to their satisfaction. Mr. Hayes had his notice and I had mine, and we were slated for the first day.

On the appointed day, we were there early, leaving Mrs. Theobold, who was not scheduled until the next day, to take care of the store. Even so, we were not the first. Four or five cars and trucks were already lined up in what had been Mr. Billy Gusto's field across the road, so I stopped at the entrance and let Mr. Hayes out and then went on and parked at the end of the row.

Although everything around it had been leveled, the graveyard had not been touched, except for some stakes the government men had driven to guide the excavation work. The line of trees across the back cast long shadows in the early sun. Here and there crepe myrtle blazed with color. The grave markers were mostly thin slabs of stone rounded at the top, originally white, but stained now and weathered gray. A few of the newer ones were blocks of rough dark granite with a space polished out for the inscription. This uniformity was not by design but simply due to the fact that the markers had been ordered through the store and Mr. Hayes offered a limited selection.

The one exception, of course, was the centaur on the Posers' lot. Somewhere in transit from the Mountains of Thessaly to Zions Cause, Kentucky, the features of that centaur had taken on the unmistakable likeness of Odie—pinched face, buck teeth, jug ears and all—and it stood there a wonder to many, an outrage to some, a comfort to the family, and to Will, the father of them all, a source of constant and immense satisfaction.

The Posers' lot was directly in front of the entrance, so you could not miss it. Will was there when I came in, reared back in a cane-bottomed kitchen chair as if he planned to make a day of it, which of course he did. His hair had gone white now, and he didn't quite fill up his clothes anymore, but his eyes still twinkled and he had a wide grin going.

"Ain't he a sight, now?" he said, but I was uncertain whether he was talking about Odie—or rather the centaur; I suppose there was no difference in his mind anymore—or Herman, who'd carved it and was sitting now on its base stone smiling shyly out from under his hat brim.

The Blackburn lot was the next one back. It was the largest and was almost filled, because there was a bunch of Blackburns both above and below ground. Old Mrs. Blackburn, who had personally experienced one of the healing miracles, was standing there with her hands on her wide hips, looking

our way, and one of her sons, Rile, who, though middle-aged
and with a family of his own, was still at her beck and call, as
they all were. As I moved over to speak to them, she pulled
me close and whispered that they ought never to have been
allowed to stick that up where everybody would have to see it,
that it was a nasty, vulgar, heathen thing and not fit for women
and children to look at, echoing, still, Mrs. Gusto, who had
started it all by confusing centaurs with satyrs.

I slipped away as soon as I could, spoke to one or two
others, and came to join Mr. Hayes at our lot. He was standing
where one day he had intended to lie, between them, Amanda
Hayes, his wife and my aunt, and Susan Wells, my mother.

Except for the inscriptions on the stones, the graves were
identical; he had seen to that. Maybe he could not control
what went on inside him, but he could make sure there was no
outward show. He tended the graves himself, personally, and
always had, taking an afternoon away from his business—not
the store, that had long since become not even just a sideline,
only a hobby to him—to come here and do whatever was
needed. He could have hired it done, or I could have done it,
after all they were mine, too, but that didn't suit him.

I never knew either of them, except through others—not
him, he never spoke of them. Mrs. Hayes they remembered as
a bitter woman who died of consumption at the age of thirty-
five, convinced of betrayal. Susan, her niece or younger sister,
nobody knew for sure, who came at the last to look after her
and after him, was by all accounts peculiar.

Her peculiarity took the form of not exactly a denial of, but
certainly an extreme lack of concern with, the external affairs
of this world. Given a routine, even a complex one such as

housekeeping, she would do it and do it well, because what did it matter to her how long it took to scrub a pot or a floor as long as she was not required to be consciously involved. Or given nothing to do, she would sit for hours, motionless, as if somewhere in there she had reached up and flipped off the switch because her body wasn't going to be needed for a while.

Physically, she was not unattractive. Years later, I found a photograph among his papers. She is thin, but not emaciated. Her face is long and her cheeks are hollow, but her chin is strong and has a faint cleft. I am told that her hair, dark in the picture, was deep auburn and in sunlight was dazzling.

In spite of, maybe because of, her peculiarity, she was universally liked. It was all one-sided. She herself was incapable of personal relationships, and everyone came to understand that. And Mr. Hayes, too. He was bound to, even before the rest. He was always ahead of them.

Even so, he let it happen, or maybe he had no control over it, was unaware until it was too late. After all, it was his first experience—and his last. Whatever the case, he was possessed; and Mrs. Hayes, lying on her deathbed, sensed it, read whatever signs there were and, lusting after one last humiliation, disregarded what she would have known better than anybody else and accused them of betrayal, directly, and to anybody else she could find to listen. Her ultimate humiliation, although I suppose she was never aware of it, was that no one believed her.

Oh, they came to believe in his possession, they could read signs, too, but not betrayal. So when Mrs. Hayes died and Susan stayed on, they accepted it. Because they knew Susan. And they knew him.

But they didn't know that preacher, not even his name. He just appeared out of nowhere one day riding a little mule, and before they even had time to think about it, Mr. Hayes was furnishing him bed and board and they had built him a brush arbor and he was holding meetings and performing healing miracles.

At first, they looked upon him as a Special Messenger from Above, and on the strength of this view, they built the church to commemorate the event. But after what later transpired, they were just as convinced that he was a fraud and a scoundrel and worse, a manifestation of that old deluder Satan, for as someone pointed out, the Devil can quote Scripture to his purposes and perform miracles, too. But the healings were real and permanent and irrefutable, and in time they seriously eroded the Deluder theory, yet failed to re-establish the Special Messenger one. It afforded them years of discussion and argument, though never in the presence of Mr. Hayes and rarely in mine.

Whatever the source, he possessed the gift, and most certainly was possessed by it, was squeezed and twisted into what they saw, something more and less than a man. But somewhere he was born, grew up, laughed, played, maybe went to school, maybe learned the rudiments of a trade. Surely he was loved by someone, was maybe even capable of it himself. Then somewhere in there he would have come to the realization that he had the gift.

Or maybe, and this is more likely, the preaching came first. He had the calling, or thought he did, which amounts to the same thing, and set himself to learn how to do it, finding in the process that what he said didn't matter so much as the way he said it, that rhythm and tone of voice worked better than coherent and logical argument, which he would not have been strong on, anyway. And then maybe he found out that the way he looked at people helped, too, and the way he used those big hands, weaving and waving and smacking into things. And then one day in the middle of it all and everything just right, he happened to lay one of those big hands on somebody and a miracle took place.

He would not have known how it happened, what it was he had done to bring it about, but it must have given him such a sense of fulfillment that just stirring them with preaching would never by itself satisfy him again. So he would have tried to repeat it. And he would have failed, because it was only by chance that he got it right the first time. But he would have had to keep trying. And maybe when he was just at the point of desperation, the conviction came upon him that the power would not be handed out for nothing, that the miracle was only a sample of what could be his if he could just find the right price. And the price he decided to offer was to forsake what claim he still had left on the world and deny the demands of the flesh. So maybe that was when he began the withdrawal and fasting and prayer. And maybe that began to work, because he believed it would. And when sometimes it didn't, he would add something else: the lacerations of those hands, and wearing that heavy coat and stiff collar and tie in the heat of summer, because he wouldn't have known about hair shirts.

So by the time he appeared in front of the store that day, he had it all worked out and knew what he was doing, even if they didn't. And there was Mr. Hayes, waiting for him on the store porch, nursing a hopeless passion; and Susan, back there somewhere in the living quarters behind the store, with the switch cut off; and the rest of them, ready and willing, without even knowing what part they would need to play.

So he had them build him that brush arbor there next to the store, and come and let him work his spell on them, and bring their sick and afflicted so he could perform the miracles. And Mr. Hayes, watching it all from the store porch, was taken by a wild hope and stepped in and demanded a miracle of his own, took him away and into the house to Susan, who was already in bed because it was long after dark, and left him to it and went back to the store porch to wait, with nothing on his mind maybe but the bright vision of a whole Susan. Having watched him for two days, Mr. Hayes would have understood that he was not whole either, so he would not have worried that he would have even recognized a temptation of the flesh much less succumbed to one. But he was wrong.

At first, he would have had his mind on working the miracle. He would have sat there on the side of her bed with those big hands cupped around her head, commanding her, maybe not fully understanding the nature of her infirmity, even though he had had plenty of time to see it for himself and on top of that Mr. Hayes had told him; not understanding either that it took both of them to make the miracle work and he was one short, even though her eyes were open and looking at him. So there would have been the frustration. And there she was, or rather her body, in her night clothes, prone, passive, pliant. Maybe he misread that look for one of willingness, even invitation. And then there was his long denial, and he still a young man, in his thirties they judged, so the drive was still there and strong, however sublimated. Maybe the urge came suddenly, took him by surprise, and she would not have helped him by offering resistance, so that before he even had time to confront it, he was already overwhelmed; overwhelmed and consequently destroyed, because all he had was the gift and the gift depended upon denial. That realization would soon have come to him.

He was gone the next morning, vanished without a trace. So they built the church in commemoration because then they knew only about the miracles. Later, after the church had been finished and dedicated, they found out what Mr. Hayes had been tormented by for some time: Susan was with child. There was, of course, much speculation. Mr. Hayes knew the straight of it, though he kept it to himself. With the birth it was resolved. The resemblance was too strong, even to the hands, which the rest of me never quite caught up with.

Susan died a few days after I was born. I was claimed by the women, had been in fact almost from the moment of birth, it being obvious that Susan didn't have the strength, much less the presence of mind, to do for me; and Mr. Hayes, they thought, wouldn't want to, or, if he did, know how to, being a man. There were enough wet nurses among them, and they all took a turn. Who I would finally wind up with was settled by Mr. Hayes, who stepped in and asserted his claim, although for the first few years, until Mrs. Theobold came on a permanent basis, he hired one or another of them to come and help look after me. Why he claimed me is no mystery: I was at least half Susan's. And if the way I looked bothered him, he never let me know it.

Mr. Hayes had wanted to get to the graveyard early that morning. There was no need to ask why. That new site was never going to hold the same claim on him as the old one had, and he needed some time. I needed some time myself, not only for the graveyard but to let go of the rest of it. Those places which marked so many events in my life and which lent substance to their memory would soon be covered by a sheet of water, featureless and sterile, evoking nothing. Standing there between the two graves, a captive of the past, he didn't notice me come up, so I sat down in the grass and surrendered to memories of my own.

So when Will hollered, we both jumped. He and Herman were standing on the base stone of the centaur, hanging onto the part that was Odie and leaning out to look down the road. We must have been hearing the sounds of engines and the clanking of treads for some time without being conscious of them, for they were clear enough now.

Coming around the bend in the road was a regular parade. In the lead was a power shovel, looking, with its boom raised, like some variety of yellow dinosaur. Behind that was a dump truck with a row of heads wearing hard hats sticking up out of the bed. Then came cars and pickup trucks and finally a flat-bed with its edges lined with people and legs dangling off all around. The dump truck and crew had come from the dam through New Zion to Zions Cause Church, where the power shovel had been left after finishing the new graves, and it looked as if everybody along the way had joined in. They were making good time, raising a fine cloud of dust in the process.

As it came abreast of the entrance, that shovel suddenly slewed around in a square turn and stopped, engine racing, blocking the road. The dump truck, close behind, locked its wheels, managing to stop just in time, those heads in the back disappearing like falling dominoes. The cars and trucks following had no time to do anything but go bouncing across the road ditch and into Mr. Gusto's field, that flatbed losing a good part of its load as it left the road.

Before the dust had time to settle, the passenger door of that dump truck flew open and a man jumped out, jammed on a yellow hard hat which he must have lost when the truck stopped, marched over to the power shovel and waited while the operator took his time shutting it down. With the engine stopped, we could hear the hollering coming from the cars and trucks out there in the field and from the road ditch where that flatbed had dumped most of its load. The man from the dump truck, who turned out to be the foreman, caught a handhold somewhere on that power shovel and swung up to stand on the tread.

"Now, Buford," he said to the shovel operator, "you want to watch yourself. Somebody could of got hurt just now."

"It ain't up to me to watch," the operator said. "I got this shovel to run. You was behind me. You ought to watch."

The foreman looked out at the cars and trucks unloading now and at those from the flatbed getting up out of the road ditch, brushing themselves off, and back at the dump truck where men were climbing out over the sides of the bed and handing out pickaxes and shovels.

"Well," he said, "no harm done, I reckon."

"None at all," Mr. Hayes said to me but loud enough for others to hear, "not if you discount broke axle springs and tore britches, not to mention the skin left in that road ditch and on the inside of that truck bed."

"Well, all right," the shovel operator said, "where do you want me to start?"

"Just hang on a minute, will you? I'll let you know."

But the operator had noticed the centaur now and jumped out of his seat and was leaning out the front of the shovel cab, pointing at it.

"What the hell is that thing?"

The foreman said, "Watch it, Buford, it's women here."

"It's Odie," Will said. He was still standing on the base stone with his arm around Odie's waist.

The operator said, "Well, I'll be damned."

The foreman said, "Now, Buford."

The operator said, "Looks like a horse."

"Just that part back there," Will said. "The front here is my boy Odie."

The operator said, "Well, I'll be goddamned."

"Buford!"

By now the crew from the dump truck were bunched in front of the entrance, shovels and pickaxes sticking out in all directions, yellow hard hats twisting back and forth together between centaur and power shovel as they followed the exchange. That crowd from the field was beginning to drift across the road, filling in any empty space it could find, trying to decide where it ought to look to find out what was going on.

The foreman stepped to the front of the shovel tread. "Now, folks," he said, "you all are going to have to stand back out of the way, now. We don't want nobody hurt. Billy, run turn the truck around, and somebody go with him and bring them rope slings out of the front. What we want to do, folks, is pass them slings under the belly of that thing and use the boom of the shovel here to lift it right out of there and set it in the truck. Mister, you and your buddy there are going to have to get down off of there. Hold it, Buford!"—because the operator was already trying to start up that power shovel—"I told you I'd tell you when I was ready!"

They got the slings in place and the power shovel moved into the entrance far enough to hook them on. Will and Herman kept darting in and out to make sure everything was all right.

"Now, Buford," the foreman said, "what you want to do is when I tell you bring your boom up slow and easy. Then you want to back out and bring her around to the truck, and then hold up, you hear me, until I can get in there and watch you down with it. Boys, some of you take aholt and steady it on the way; we don't want it to swing on us. Mister, you and your friend there try to keep out of the way; we know what we're doing. All right, Buford, easy now."

He stooped down, watching the base of the statue, his hand raised, index finger making circles in the air. As the slack in the slings was taken up, the engine picked up speed and the shovel rocked forward on its treads under the load. The centaur rose slowly to about chest height, one man holding onto each leg, and stopped with a jerk when the foreman drew his hand across his throat. Then, following his signals, the shovel backed into the road again and began to swing the centaur toward the truck, the four men steadying it facing each other so that the two in front were walking backward.

I guess it was our fault as much as anybody's. We all saw it, the road ditch they would have to cross, but nobody said anything. The two walking backward went down first, losing their hold on the centaur as the ground dropped out from under them. The other two tried to stop, digging in their heels. Maybe that operator had his mind on something else and didn't see what was happening or hear the hollering. Anyway, he kept the boom moving toward the truck, so when the two left holding finally had to let go, the centaur took a big swing and one leg caught the side of the truck bed and snapped off at the fetlock.

The operator saw that and jerked the boom in the other direction, in perfect time to help that centaur on its back swing. The two men getting up out of the road ditch had just enough time to turn around when the two on the edge hollered before that centaur caught all four and knocked them back into the graveyard and into that crowd which had followed them around. For some of them who had been on that flatbed truck it was the second time in less than an hour they had hit the dirt, so maybe they were coming to expect it.

In the middle of it all the foreman gave up waving and hollering to no avail and ran to the shovel and right up the side of it and into the cab, as if there were steps and that tread was the first one, and, reaching around the operator to get to the controls, shut it down. The centaur, with nothing to check it now that it had cleared out a path for itself, was making long, looping swings, stopping in midair at the top of each and jerking the shovel when it started back down.

Some of the crew ran in to stop it, not those four who had tried to steady it, they had not yet got untangled from that crowd, and besides, maybe they had had enough for a while. Will went to the truck and located that snapped-off hoof and brought it to Herman to look at. The shovel operator was waving his arms and hollering at the foreman, though with the noise of the crowd we had to guess at what he was saying. It looked like the foreman was trying to calm him down. Those four and that crowd finally began to untangle and get up, the two who had been in front holding their chests where the centaur had caught them. Mr. Hayes, who had watched it all from his spot between the two graves, turned and looked at me. After a while he said, "You can add to them broke springs and tore britches and them skinned knees and elbows, one busted centaur and two crushed chests."

"All right, now, everybody," the foreman said. He was still in the cab of the shovel, leaning out the front. "Listen now, folks. You see what can happen if you don't stand back out of the way? We're just lucky somebody didn't get hurt. So back up now like I told you and let us get on with our business. Mister," he said to Will, who with Herman was trying to fit that broken hoof back on the leg stump, "don't worry about it, Mister, the guvmint will make it right. All right, boys, what we're going to do now is I'm going to get in the truck, and I want three or four of you in there with me. Then Buford here is going to raise her up a couple more feet and . . ." But we lost the rest of it because that power shovel started up again.

It went without further incident, the loading of the centaur and then the base stone into the truck. Then the foreman coaxed that power shovel back into the graveyard where it began to bite chucks out of Odie's grave, piling the dirt along one side. On the other side, those yellow hard hats lined up with their tools, waiting, looking like an honor guard at parade rest. The crowd filled in behind them. Will stood at the foot of the grave but well back, turning that hoof over in his hands, and Herman behind him. The foreman paced up and down between that honor guard and the grave, stopping now and then to inspect the work and nodding encouragement to the shovel operator, who was paying him no mind.

The shovel opened a trench maybe a yard deep, and maybe twice that wide, the length of the grave and then some. Then it shut down, and that crew of hard hats started up and took off the rest of the overburden and trenched around the sides and ends of the coffin, keeping that crowd at bay by throwing the dirt in their direction.

The foreman, standing at the head of the grave now and watching the work, explained. "How we handle it depends on what kind of shape it's in. If it's still sound, why all we have to do is throw them slings around it and haul it right out of there. But now if it's rotted, why then we have to box it and that takes some time. Now this one here don't look in too bad a shape. How long has she been in there, Mister?"

"Five years come September," Will told him.

"October," Herman said, low.

"What?" Will said.

"He was struck the last of September. We buried him the first day of October."

"A day wouldn't make all that much difference," the foreman said. "All right, boys. What does she look like?"

One of them down there thumped the coffin. It made a dull sound. "Not too bad," he said. "A little soft, maybe."

"What about the bottom?"

"Can't tell. Have to raise her up first."

Everybody got still, waiting. We could hear grunting and

thumping and them talking to each other, though we couldn't make out anything.

"Well," the foreman said. "Do we need to box it or not?"

"Maybe."

"What's that supposed to mean?"

"Hell, I don't know. I ain't no expert. Come look for yourself."

The foreman looked at that crowd and shook his head. Then he dropped into the hole, and right away we could hear thumping. Then that stopped and they boosted him out. He stood up and dusted off his hands, held them up to his nose and then took out a blue bandana and began to wipe them. Finally, he made up his mind.

"Put them slings on her, boys," he said. "Buford, fire up!"

But he had cut it too fine. Maybe if all had gone right, he would have got by. But he knew what he had to work with, so he ought to have known better than to chance it. They got the coffin out of the grave. They even got it out of the graveyard and into position over the bed of that dump truck. But then without waiting to be told, the operator began to lower it.

"Hold it, Buford!" the foreman hollered, dancing up and down and sawing his throat with his hand. "Let us get in there first!"

The operator didn't just stop the boom, he reversed it. The jerk was too much. There was a dull crack of wood, and then the bottom of the coffin opened up like a trap door and dropped what was left of Odie into the truck bed. We saw him go in, and we heard him hit bottom, and now we could smell him, or maybe it was just our imagination.

There was not a sound from that crowd, except for an in-drawn breath when it happened. There was just the clucking of the shovel engine at idle. The foreman climbed up the side of the truck and looked over into the bed. After a while, he turned and motioned to the crew, but nobody moved. He looked at them awhile, then at us, then he looked into the bed again. Finally, he looked at the shovel operator and held up a hand, thumb down. The operator lowered what was left of the coffin into the truck. The foreman climbed up and straddled the side of the bed and leaned over and unhooked the slings from the shovel. Then he slipped to the ground and got into the cab.

"All right," he said to the crew, "you four men right there, load up and bring your shovels. Come on, Billy, let's go."

They stood on the running boards, two on each side, holding on to the truck with one hand and on to their shovels with the other. The truck started up and eased off down the road to Zions Cause, picking up speed as it turned the bend.

Then that crowd let its breath out and began to tell each other what had happened as they saw it.

Rile Blackburn, who had come over to our side to watch and was standing right in front of us, said what maybe others were thinking. "I guess it's a good thing they brought a dump truck. Now they won't even have to touch him, just raise the bed and slide him right in."

We were looking for Will and Herman, Mr. Hayes and I. We spotted them crossing the road headed for their truck and called to them to wait. We caught up to them next to the power shovel. The operator had switched it off and was sitting up there with his feet propped up on the edge of the cab, taking his ease. Will was holding that broken hoof, still turning it over in his hands.

Mr. Hayes was breathing hard through his nose. He didn't say anything right away, maybe he wasn't able to, just patted Will on the shoulder for a while. Finally, he said, "I'm sorry, Will."

Will looked up from that broken hoof. "He said they would make it right," he said. "And even if they don't, Herman thinks he can fix it back on."

Mr. Hayes stared at him, his mouth opening and closing but nothing coming out. After a while, he turned to me, speaking loud enough for everybody to hear.

"Go to the store and get some tools. Then go out to the saw-mill and get a truck and bring back some men with you. Wait!" he said, as I was leaving. "Bring a shotgun, too."

I went on to the car with him still hollering.

"When you get back, I want you to stand here and hold it on this damned fool in this power shovel, and if he makes a move toward our lot, I want you to shoot him!"

As I drove past on my way to the store, he was still hollering.

"Aim at his neck. If you can blow his head off, maybe that will stop him quicker!"

So we moved our own, Mr. Hayes and I, with some help from the mill hands. Actually, as I was to discover, it was not really all that necessary because they were both sealed in steel boxes so we could have safely left it to the government crew. But it was not safety that Mr. Hayes was concerned about, and I could understand his feelings.

It took us most of the day, because Mr. Hayes didn't use the mill hands any more than he had to, but he and I did most of the digging and covering ourselves. We finished just before dark. The new graves were arranged just like the old ones with a space for him in between. He had ordered a new marker, and it was already in place, a single block of granite which stretched the width of the three graves. Between the inscriptions for them, there was one for him with the second date left out. When I went to take the hands back to the sawmill and pick up the car, I left him standing between them again. It was full dark when I got back to the store; even so, Mrs. Theobold and I had to wait supper on him.

Rile, as it turned out, was wrong about the way they would handle Odie. Those who followed them said that in the bed of that dump truck they had stacks of ready-built box sides and ends. They said they nailed a box together in there, in private, and put Odie in it. And that foreman kept everybody away, especially Will and Herman, until it was done. Then they said they let down the tailgate and handed the box out and lowered it into the new grave with all the respect you could ask for.

They did tip the truck bed to slide out the centaur and base stone. When it came to setting them up, they said the foreman turned everything over to Herman and worked right along with the others under his direction. As they were easing the centaur down over those pins in the base stone, Herman slipped that broken hoof in place and the weight locked it there. It's still there. You have to look hard to see the break line even if you know where to look. They said when it was all over, Will asked for the paper he was supposed to sign and signed it, which must have taken a load off that foreman's mind.

The rest of the move fell way behind schedule, stretching out to more than a week what was expected to take at the most three days, because that foreman insisted that just about every one of them be boxed. That dump truck made only a couple of trips each day, passing the store on its slow, solemn way to the church with only a half dozen or so of boxes and about the same number of hard hats and shovel handles showing above the top of the bed and maybe as many cars and trucks following along behind. Any who happened to be watching from the store porch would bare their heads until they were past, feeling the need to show respect.

The last day, Mr. Hayes and I talked about going back for one final look. Before we could get around to it, we were sent for, or rather he was. We were at the table when we heard a car stop and somebody come into the store in a hurry. Mrs. Theobold, who was waiting on us, went out to see about it and brought back one of those Blackburns. He didn't look old enough to have a license to drive, and probably wasn't, which wouldn't have bothered him, and he was short on breath as if he had run all the way.

"Uncle Rile wants to know if you can come out to the graveyard right away," he told Mr. Hayes.

"What for?"

"They found somebody."

"What do you mean, found somebody?"

"Somebody who wasn't supposed to be there," he was hollering some now, "and Uncle Rile wants you to come look!"

Mr. Hayes' coffee cup had stopped halfway between his saucer and his mouth. He looked surprised to find it there. If it had been filled with nitroglycerin, he wouldn't have set it down with more care or taken more time about it. Without looking up, he said, "All right, tell him I'll be there directly."

It was that shovel operator again. Somebody, probably some little ones playing, had taken some of those marker stakes and reset them back next to that line of trees where nobody used. The operator, without waiting to be told or deigning to ask, had begun digging there. By the time they noticed it and stopped him, he had already turned up a skull. It was only by sheer chance he missed the rest of it. That shovel had come within a fraction of an inch of it in places, but it was left intact.

Herman and those wise hands of his, and with all of them watching, had uncovered the rest of it and found the cross. It was not until he had finished and set the skull back in place and cleaned the cross and laid it on the breast bone that Rile was struck by a notion, Will, too, when Rile explained it to him. Mrs. Blackburn, after some one of them had gone and got her, was convinced that it couldn't be anyone else.

"Just look how tall. And look at them hand bones. And I'm satisfied that's the very cross; after all, I'm one of the few that seen it up close. I say it's him."

Everybody was waiting on Mr. Hayes. He took his time about it. Finally, he said, "It could be anybody."

Mrs. Blackburn opened her mouth and drew in a breath, but Mr. Hayes wasn't finished yet. "There's nothing special about that cross."

"But you got to admit it all fits," Rile said. "The right size, that cross, the time, too, maybe." He turned to the foreman. "How long would you say he's been there?"

"No telling. Could be ten years, could be a hundred. Depends on a lot of things. We uncovered one once that had been there seventy-five years. Coffin had a glass plate. You could still see his face. Looked like he was sleeping. Course, he fell apart when we went to move him. This here, now, no sign of a coffin, so meat and clothes wouldn't last all that long."

"But it could be twenty years. And if it ain't him, who is it?"

Rile was getting close, but he still had not hit on the right question.

Mrs. Blackburn said, "I'm well satisfied it's him."

"It could be anybody," Mr. Hayes said. "It's an old grave-yard."

"And if it is him," Rile said, "how did he get here?"

There. That was it. That was what had been bothering me ever since we had passed through that crowd and Rile had showed us and said what he thought. It bothered me, too, that Mr. Hayes evaded him.

"It's an old graveyard," he said again. "Maybe it was some-body just passing through and one of them died. This might have been the best they could do for him."

But then Mrs. Blackburn went too far and said, "It even looks like him."

That drew a snicker from the crowd and destroyed any credi-bility she might have had. The foreman looked at Mr. Hayes and shook his head. Rile gave a sheepish grin and said, "Aw, Momma."

But she was not that far off. Believing as he had, he would have taken only enough nourishment to keep him going. And those who had been there twenty years ago had remarked upon his thinness, even that he looked like a death's head. The re-semblance was undoubtedly what had first struck Rile, though maybe it took the placing of the cross to trigger his awareness of it. But hearing it spoken aloud made him see the foolishness in it. And maybe Mrs. Blackburn, weighing the reaction, was having second thoughts, too, though she was never going to be entirely convinced.

Mr. Hayes, ahead now and knowing it, looked at the foreman and asked, "What will you do?"

"Whatever suits you. He ain't on the list. Like you say, it could be anybody, and it ain't much way of finding out who. If you tell me to, I'll just cover him back up and forget it. And may he rest in peace. On the other hand, I was sent here to empty this place, and that's what I'd like to do."

It was Rile who decided it. "It's plenty of room at the new place not assigned to nobody."

"All right. Trench him out, boys. And two of you go get some boxing. Buford, take that shovel out of here and park it across the road. And see if you can manage not to dig up anything else, you hear me?"

We had already turned to go, were leaving, when the foreman asked, "What about this here cross?"

Mr. Hayes kept on walking until he heard me say, "I'll take it."

He stopped then, but didn't turn around, just stood there facing ahead until I passed him, then followed me on to the car.

We sat a long time on the store porch that night, with an uneasy silence between us and Mr. Hayes waiting for me to ask the question. He would not have tried to evade me as he had Rile. He would have known better. After all, he had taught me. Or maybe honor or justice or, what was more important to him, fairness would have compelled him to answer. If I found I needed to ask.

Oh, he would have been capable, I had no doubt about that, in hot blood, certainly, as most of us are. It might not even have been his first. It was speculated that in his youth he had fought Spaniards in Cuba, had ridden with Teddy Roosevelt up San Juan Hill. Even if the latter was not true, he had certainly seen action somewhere; he knew too much about it. Then, too, for him at least, there had been provocation enough and to spare.

But say he did. Say he left the store porch that night and went in and found them, or rather him. And without considering whether it was an act of volition on his part any more than on hers (he knew neither of them was whole), say he stepped to the sitting room and took from the wall one of that pair of pistols that, along with that sword, he had brought back from the war, and loaded it and went back and shot him. And then say he went out and caught that little mule he had come on and loaded him on it and a shovel and led it out to the graveyard. And there in a shallow grave back next to that line of trees where he was pretty sure he would not be disturbed or the grave even noticed, say he buried him and then ran that little mule off or otherwise got rid of it and came away scot-free. Say that is what happened or something like it, what then? Would it make any difference? Would it negate or diminish or change what he was, or was to me?

And if there must be justice, well, he didn't go scot-free. He lost Susan. And, if that was not enough, he was serving a life sentence, had already served twenty years of it, of having constantly before him the image of her violator, every time he looked at me. It was a harsh penalty. If he was guilty. But I didn't know for sure that he was. And I didn't need to know, didn't even want to know.

Blood, they say, is thicker than water. That is only literally true. Blood, even given the opportunity, would not have claimed me, fed and clothed me, educated me and most of all cared for me. Put to the test, love is the only thing that matters or prevails.

I had kept him waiting a long time, way too long. I needed to put his mind to rest, but I couldn't think of any good way to do it. Finally, I just said something that had been rattling around in my head.

"You know, I've been thinking. Suppose a stranger happened up on that old graveyard with all those empty graves. Do you reckon he might think it was Resurrection day and he had missed it?"

It wasn't much, but then it didn't take much for him. He was always out in front.

When the Fire Comes
[1945]

"Why east?" Old John Bumpus demanded. "Why was it Jonah chose out the *east* side of Nineveh to set and wait so as to witness the destruction? Because it was a hill there? Well, of course it was! But it was a hill on the west side, too. Nineveh was in a valley with hills on both sides. So why east, then? I'll tell you why. So he could smell the smoke! The wind would have been from the west there just like it is here, and on the east, see, the smoke would drift right over him, the smoke and the wailing and the noise of gnashing teeth. He could hear it and smell it and know for certain that they got what was coming to them."

I had been gone nearly four years, most of that time in Europe with the war, and now here I was with the rest of them in the rear of Mr. Hayes' new store in New Zion listening to Old John holding forth just as if I had never been away. Well, almost.

"Now, John," somebody said, "you know as well as I do, it didn't actually come off."

"And a damned shame, too, if you ask me!—That bunch of snotty-nosed A-rabs running around hollering We repent! We repent! and him left there in the hot sun ay god and not so much as a whiff of brimstone to make up for all he'd been through. But the day is coming, it's a-coming I tell you, when crying and taking on won't work. And when it does, I hope to be right where Jonah was, on the east side!"

"Well," somebody else said, "I hope it's Nineveh you're figuring on, because anywheres east of here is going to put you in about forty foot of water."

That was not true, but nobody disputed it. New Zion was a good two miles from Kentucky Lake. Zions Cause, that fragment that had not been swallowed by the lake, consisted now of only a few residences, and I suppose no longer could be said to have tangible existence. Yet all of them had been born and brought up in Zions Cause and their minds were so imprinted by its coordinates that the notion of "here" was always going to be Zions Cause rather than wherever they happened to be. And it was true that anywhere east of Zions Cause was more than somewhat wet.

"Watch it!" Old John warned whoever it was. "They laughed at Elisha and he sicked bears on them and they et them."

We called him Old John not because he was so old, rather because he was so familiar. After a feckless youth, he had made it one of his prime missions in life to haunt our old store in Zions Cause and now moving with the times had transferred his operations to the new one. Consequently, everyone saw considerably more of him than of each other.

Old John was, you might say, a prisoner of Grace. While still a young man, he had unintentionally and indeed against his will become a born-again Christian—"got sanctified," as he put it—and had been compelled by conscience thereafter into a more sober way of life, a condition that, whether consciously or not, he resented bitterly. Thus, Old John harbored an abiding grievance against the world in general, and in particular against those who were free to enjoy its pleasures, and sought solace in Scripture, being especially fond of those passages of an apocalyptic nature.

Old John never married. Women, or the pursuit thereof, was one of the things he gave up after his conversion. And like the fowls of the air, he sowed not, neither did he reap. But work wasn't something he gave up, too, for the simple reason that it was not his to give. He had lived off his parents until they died, and then soon after, when the lake took his land, his settlement with the government was generous enough to provide him a small house in New Zion and enough left over to keep him, if he was careful, for several years if not for life. Thus he had plenty of time to ponder the Scriptures and to propound his thoughts at the store, and even if he did tend to identify a shade too closely with the prophets of doom, nobody really minded because his approach was invariably original and interesting.

"It ain't no bears no more, John, except in a zoo, and they ain't going to bother nobody. Just don't you go sicking Miss Daisy on me. I'd lots rather be et up than broke off. I ain't near as brave as you."

Daisy Goins, Miss Daisy as she had been called for several years now, was shaped like a wedge, mostly head, shoulders and bosom, and then tapering off from there. It was theorized that everything she ate went to breasts and the rest of her had to do without. She was musically inclined, more or less, and had once been the pianist at Zions Cause Church and as such was the subject of much discussion, not because of her musical ability but because she rarely rose from the piano stool that her dress was not caught in her crack, and there it would remain for the rest of the service.

I recalled one of many store porch discussions from earlier years which I suppose the remark referenced.

"I can't believe that she don't know it. Surely she can feel it."

"She can't feel it. She backed into me once in a crowd and, let me tell you, that thing is as hard as iron. Why, I bet she can tighten them cheeks and crack a hickernut! She ain't about to feel no little old flimsy piece of dress material."

"Maybe it's got a mind of its own and just snaps shut on anything that comes handy. You're lucky it didn't snap shut on you. Now wouldn't that a-been embarrassing—all hung up like mating dogs right there in front of everybody."

Despite being more than moderately top-heavy, Miss Daisy was considered pretty as a girl and was now as a mature woman often characterized as handsome, yet she, like Old John, had remained single, never, I suppose, having found anybody who measured up to her standards of order, for she was a formidable duster and straightener, both in her own life and that of anyone else who wasn't careful, and always had been, that trouble she used to have with her dress, which I suppose she was never aware of and which a style change to tighter underwear had long since taken care of anyway, being the only exception.

Miss Daisy was of an age with Old John and in similar circumstances, perhaps a little better off financially. The fact that they were next-door neighbors was bound to cause talk but it was all in fun. Nobody seriously believed ill of either of them.

"After a remark like that," Old John said, "I can see bears ain't going to be near good enough for you. It'll take fire—fire like Elijah called down that time and consumed a hundred men and two captains!"

I wondered how Old John would handle it if he ever came face to face with the results of the real holocaust and said so to Mr. Hayes at the supper table that night.

"I know you don't want to talk about it," he said, speaking not to the thought itself but to the reason for its occurrence, "and I can understand that. I can only tell you what you know already: That's part of it, too. And you've got somehow to fit that in with the rest and go on from there."

Well, he had managed it in his time, but then he had not had to cope with the results of firebombing or view the crematoria at Cracow.

"As for John Bumpus," Mr. Hayes said, moving on, "maybe he will be lucky and never have to deal with anything more than a lively imagination."

It was not to be. And coming as it did so close on the heels of our discussion it made me feel against all reason that I was somehow responsible.

At eleven-thirty the phone rang. I was in bed but not asleep. I hurried downstairs hoping I could catch it before it woke Mr. Hayes or Mrs. Theobold, but as I lifted the receiver he was already coming down the steps. It was Old John asking for him. He took the receiver and spoke his name and then for the next few minutes all he could do was listen. I couldn't understand what was being said but I did gather it was urgent, whatever it was, or at least Old John thought so. Finally, he ran down and Mr. Hayes was able to talk. "All right, John, we'll come. You just go on back home, now, and wait for us. We'll be there directly."

"It's Miss Daisy," Mr. Hayes said as we went back upstairs to get dressed. "He's afraid something has happened to her. He says he knocked on her door a little while ago and couldn't get an answer."

"I suppose it never crossed his mind she might be asleep."

"He says the lights are on."

"Well, maybe she just forgot to turn them off."

"Miss Daisy?"

"I suppose you're right. What about the windows? Could he see anything through—No, she would have drawn the shades at the first sign of dark."

"On the door panel, too."

"Well, if he was all that concerned, why didn't he just break the glass and reach in and open it?"

"What do you think he wants us for?" Mr. Hayes said. "Anyway, you still haven't asked the real question."

"What question is that?"

"What kind of business did John Bumpus have with Miss Daisy at eleven o'clock at night!"

The one public phone in New Zion was located in a booth in front of Big Jack's new filling station—styled HEDDIN'S SERVICE AND REPAIR—out on the highway. Old John had called from there, so we pulled up in front of Miss Daisy's just as he came loping down the street.

"See there!" he said, then stopped to puff. "Lights on and everything, just like I told you!"

Her lights were on all right. But not his. Would he have

gone back when he found he couldn't raise her and turned them off before going to the phone to call us? Or had he turned them off before he left on whatever business it was he had with her because he knew he was going to be away some time? I glanced at Mr. Hayes to see if he had noticed and found him looking at me for what I took to be the same reason.

Mr. Hayes got the tire tool out of the trunk and we went up the walk and the steps to the front porch with Old John at our heels, almost stepping on us in his eagerness to get on with it.

"I knocked and knocked and rattled the door," he told us. "I even hollered."

"Well," Mr. Hayes said. "We'll give it one more try. Miss Daisy!"

We waited, listening.

"Miss Daisy, it's Jim Hayes. Are you all right?"

We could hear nothing except Old John's heavy breathing behind us.

"Miss Daisy!"

"See!" Old John said. "Just like I told you!"

Mr. Hayes laid his hand on the doorknob and then snatched it back. "Good Lord!" he said. "Feel that. Careful, don't burn yourself."

I felt the knob. It was not hot enough to burn the skin, but it didn't miss it far. Old John reached between us and felt it, too. "Lord have mercy!" he said.

"It wasn't like this before?" Mr. Hayes asked him.

"I never fooled with this door. I was at the back door."

Mr. Hayes touched the glass panel. "That's hot, too!" he said and drew back to strike it with the tire tool. I caught his hand just in time. Among other things, they had taught me more than anyone should ever have to know about fire.

I got them away from in front of the door and back against the wall. Then I took the tire tool and standing well to the side myself tapped the corner of the panel. The explosion sent shards of glass across the porch and down the walk all the way to the street. I heard them hit the car. And the blast of hot air that followed burned my face as it passed.

"Wait for the fire!" I told them. But there was no following fire. There was not even smoke. Just a slight, faintly sweet, horribly familiar smell drifting through the open panel of the door.

"It's bad," I told Mr. Hayes. And then we went in.

The air was still hot and so was whatever we touched, but there was little damage, at first we thought none at all. Then we noticed the floor in front of the stove had been scorched and the padding on a footstool there had partly charred away. There was no sign of anyone.

"She ain't here!" Old John said. He brushed past us and began running around opening the doors leading to the rest of the house hollering, "Daisy! Daisy!" He disappeared into the hallway and we could hear him opening doors there and calling.

We had stopped, Mr. Hayes and I, just inside the front door. We waited there looking around while Old John searched the house. The smell was a little stronger inside but not much.

Finally, Old John came back. "She ain't anywhere," he said. Then he looked toward the stove. "Why, her chair's gone, too!"

"What chair?"

"*Her* chair. The one she set in. The one that footstool yonder belonged to. The one that table yonder with the lamp on it set beside. The one she kept drawed up to the stove, right yonder where that scorched spot is. It was a rocker. Had a padded seat and back, little chickens embroidered on them. Never liked for me to set in it. Made me use that other chair yonder. Gone, ay god!"

We went over to look. The scorched place was in the shape of a rough circle three to four feet in diameter. The lamp table and the footstool were just outside it. We could see now that the lampshade and table on the side next to the circle were scorched, too. And in the center of the circle was a small pile of black, oily-looking ashes.

"What do you make of it?" Mr. Hayes asked.

I only shook my head.

"Why didn't it spread?" he asked. "What stopped it?"

Oxygen exhaustion crossed my mind, but I knew it was not that.

He walked over and held his palm out to the stove. "Still going," he said, proving me right. Then something behind the footstool caught his attention. He bent over to pick it up, then jumped back and said, "Oh my Lord!"

It was Miss Daisy's carpet slipper. And inside was Miss Daisy's foot, burned off at the ankle.

Old John's bellow was deafening. "He's done it! God damn His soul to Hell, He's done it! He's done gone and taken her by fire!" And then his eyes rolled up and he fell to the floor.

I knelt beside him. His face was gray, but the pulse at his neck was steady. I straightened his legs and loosened his belt and shirt collar. "Shock," I told Mr. Hayes. I had seen it before. "See if you can find something to cover him up with. Then he's going to need a doctor, or at least something to quiet him down, maybe put him out for a while. And we're going to need the sheriff. And I just hope he's good at lying because nobody is ever going to believe the truth here. I see a phone on the wall next to the hall door. Maybe it's not melted inside and is still working."

By some miracle or other, it was.

The sheriff brought the doctor with him and he pumped enough sedative into Old John to lay him away for the rest of the night. We put him temporarily in Miss Daisy's bed to sleep until the sheriff was finished with us and we could take him on to our house.

"Why should he mind?" Mr. Hayes said as we covered him up. "Wasn't this where he was headed in the first place?"

When we got back to the sitting room, the doctor, who it turned out was also the country coroner, was turning the foot over in his hands and frowning. The sheriff was poking around in a cupboard in one corner of the room. "Must of been some hot in here," he said. "Here's some candles that the wax has melted right off of and left the wicks laying bare."

He continued around the room, touching things, stopping now and then to inspect some spot more closely. "Greasy scum on everything. Not much of a housekeeper."

"Miss Daisy would skin him alive," Mr. Hayes said to me.

Finally, he worked his way around to us. "Now," he said to Mr. Hayes, "we'd appreciate it if you'd just kind of fill us in on everything that happened from the time you got here till when we got here."

Mr. Hayes did. What he left out would have been of no official interest to either of them. When it came my turn, I had nothing to add.

"Well, I guess we can take it she ain't just out somewheres, because if she is, she's going to look mighty funny running around without that thing," the sheriff said, nodding toward the foot which, mercifully, the doctor was carefully wrapping in a newspaper he had taken from a magazine rack.

"Miss Daisy was a fine woman," Mr. Hayes said.

"I intended no disrespect. What I meant was, it's obvious she burnt up. Now, the question is, how did it happen?"

I wasn't about to offer an opinion. Mr. Hayes remained silent, too.

"Well, here's the way I see it. She was setting here reading, say. The stove door is open. Maybe she didn't get it closed good. Some women are like that. My wife for one. Claims loading a stove is a man's job, anyway. Well, she's setting here and the door's open a crack. A hot coal pops out and lands maybe in her lap, and before she notices, it catches her dress on fire and up she goes in flames."

Mr. Hayes said. "The stove door was shut."

"When you saw it, it was shut. Maybe the explosion blowed it shut."

"Still won't do," the doctor said. "Why was the fire confined to this one place? Why didn't it spread?"

"Lack of air," the sheriff said, repeating my nonsense. "It burnt up all the air in the room."

"Then the fire in the stove would have gone out. It didn't. Here's something else. If that little dab of ashes is what I think it is, and I guess it must be, do you have any idea how hot it would have to get to reduce bone to that?"

"Three thousand degrees," I said, "more if you wanted to be quick about it."

The doctor looked at me in some surprise. "That's right,

that's exactly right. Now how are you going to get heat like that out of an open fire fueled by clothes and a cotton-padded chair? You're not. And even if you could, how could you keep it from burning a hole right through the floor instead of just scorching it, or setting fire to that paper lampshade, or completely destroying that footstool?"

The sheriff still didn't see it. "Are you telling me," he said, "that what happened here didn't happen?"

"Not that it didn't happen. That it *couldn't* happen." The doctor looked at me to see if I agreed. "Look, I think what happened is pretty evident. She's sitting in the chair. She has one foot stretched out resting on the footstool. A ball of heat—confined heat! It wouldn't have to be fire—envelops her, consumes her and the chair, reduces them to ashes, leaves the foot that's on the footstool because it's outside the sphere of confinement. That thing doesn't radiate any of its heat, or precious little of it, and only what's actually touching it is affected—the floor, the lampshade, the table, the edge of the footstool. And then when it has done its job, it begins slowly to dissipate, gradually releasing its heat to the rest of the room, and along with the heat a greasy fog that settles on the walls and furniture, so that you think it's bad housekeeping, when everything else in this room is so tidy you can't live with it. Now, by any natural science known to me, that's not possible. Yet I believe that's what happened."

He looked at me. That was very close to the way I had seen it.

"Do you mean it was something supernatural?"

"Well, I certainly wouldn't call it natural. But I'll tell you this: It has happened before. It's rare, but not unheard of. It's mentioned in more than one treatise on forensic medicine. Not that I ever believed any of those accounts until now. It has even got a name—spontaneous human combustion—which, of course, doesn't explain anything."

"I wonder if he'd buy John Bumpus' idea of divine perversity," Mr. Hayes said to me.

"Damn it, man, you're giving me goosebumps!" the sheriff said, seeing it at last.

"Well, they're not fatal or I'd have been dead ten minutes after I walked into this room."

"Wait, now, there has to be some other explanation."

"Well, there's not, and you can see that as well as the rest of us."

"All I can see is, ain't nobody going to believe it. And when the newspapers get through with me I'll be the biggest fool in seven states. I'll tell you just what they'll do. I've seen it before. They will just keep snapping my picture till they get one with my mouth open and my eyes half-closed, looking about fifteen cents drunk, and then run it next to the shot of that burnt spot in the floor under a big headline that says, SHERIFF CLAIMS IT WAS A FIREBALL FROM THE BEYOND. And, good Lord, the inquest! There'll have to be an inquest."

"Not much way around it, I'm afraid."

"Well, what will I do? What will I say?"

"You just leave the inquest to me. I'll ask the kind of questions that will lead to your theory about a live coal popping out of the stove."

"And what about them?" he said, looking at us.

"I don't reckon we're any more eager to play the fool than you are," Mr. Hayes said.

"Anyway," the doctor said, "I wouldn't see the need to call any outside witnesses at all. You've got all the facts, haven't you?"

We left it at that and took Old John to our house and put him to bed again. We didn't go to bed ourselves. We were both too shocked to sleep. We talked about it the rest of the night, trying to make some sense out of it, but there was no way we could do that. (I even found myself telling him about some of what I had seen in the war that didn't make sense either.) And we talked about Miss Daisy, whom I had known all my life and he all of hers, and about the gap she would leave.

When Mrs. Theobold got up the next morning and found out what had happened—the sheriff's version, not the real one; no need to burden her with that—she made it very plain to us how put out she was that we hadn't called her. "There was nothing you could do," we told her. "Nothing anybody could do."

We had breakfast and were up in Old John's room when he finally woke up.

"I know why He done it," he told us. "It wasn't her He was after, it was me. She never done a wrong thing in her life, except maybe she was too interested in everything being just so, but that wasn't wrong, it was just her way. Naw, it was me. He's got His mind set against me ever doing anything that I want to do in this life."

He was propped up with pillows against the headboard of the bed, drinking the coffee that Mrs. Theobold had brought and seemed calm enough.

"And you can't beat Him. It ain't no way you can beat Him. Jonah tried to outrun Him and look where it got him. And that gourd vine he was using for shade, He even killed that. And now, this. I'll tell you one thing. If He was out to hurt me, well ay god He couldn't of found a better way!"

He talked on for a while longer and then got up and dressed and we took him home. He got out of the car and stood there looking at Miss Daisy's house. Finally, he said, "It ain't right, but I reckon I'll just have to live with it."

On the way back Mr. Hayes said, "Well, now we know."

He was referring, of course, to my question of how Old John would deal with the real thing. I had to admit, it was far better than I had done. I didn't think his way would work for me, but it might do, at least until I found something better.

The Passing
[1950]

Brother Uriah would preach him straight into Hell, and Mr. Hayes knew it, yet it was his explicit instructions that Brother Uriah was to preach his funeral.

"There are just two things I'm going to ask," he said. "I want it to be him, and I want it to be here"—meaning Zions Cause Church.

Zions Cause Church had been abandoned for nearly ten years. Mr. Hayes watched the abandonment in silence. It was not until the property was put up for sale, and immediately attracted several prospective buyers, that he stepped in: sent for Mr. Billy Gusto and Rile Blackburn and Jack Heddin, who were the trustees, and told them, "Boys, you can't sell."

"Now, Jim," Mr. Billy said, "I know you give us the land, and it was a fine thing to do, but you did give it, so now you got no say in it."

"If that's what you think, I'd advise you to read the deed. It don't say it's yours forever. Only so long as there's an active church there. Otherwise, the land comes back to me or mine."

Mr. Billy said, "We'll sue!"

"Sue and be damned."

"But we need the money," Rile said. "That new church has done run us about half again what we figured, what with adding this and adding that."

"What's your best offer?" Mr. Hayes asked.

Rile told him. He wrote out a check in that amount.

"I don't aim to cause a hardship," he told them, "but that land is rightfully mine, and I want it back."

Mr. Billy was mollified, but he was not able to get his head around simple generosity. He winked and said, "I know you, Jim Hayes. You got something in mind, now don't you?"

He did. But Mr. Billy never did understand what it was.

What it was was mere preservation. Too much of Mr. Hayes was intertwined in the church and the circumstances surrounding its establishment, and he couldn't let it go. He kept and maintained it for ten years while Mr. Billy told the others, "He's just waiting. When the price gets high enough to suit him, he'll sell"—ignoring the fact that, through what had to be accident, because even Mr. Hayes couldn't see that far into the future, he owned long stretches of other lakefront property so that the little bit the church stood on would have been beneath his notice had profit been his motive.

Six months ago, Mr. Hayes had the first attack. It was mild. Mrs. Theobold had called me at the University in Lexington, where I was in my last year of law school, but by the time I had driven the two hundred and thirty miles home, the crisis had passed. Tom Heddin, our only homegrown physician, who was around my age and who, when he had finished his training, had elected to come back and set up practice in New Zion, as I planned to do, said it was a warning.

"But at his age," he told me, "chances are another one will do for him."

"Does he know that?" I asked.

"You've been with him all your life," he said. "Have you ever been able to keep anything from him?"

It was then that Mr. Hayes gave me the instructions about who and where.

"Why him?" I asked.

"It has to be somebody. I won't ask you to just shove me into the ground, though that would suit me all right. I know you couldn't bring yourself to do that. And even if you could, Sarah wouldn't allow it, nor Mrs. Theobold. And then there are all the others who will need a funeral. And he will be honest and fair according to his own lights. I'll be content with that."

I didn't need to ask why he wanted the funeral held in Zions Cause Church; I could figure that out for myself. And where he would be buried had been settled long ago. Between them: Amanda Hayes, his wife and my aunt, and Susan Wells, his beloved Susan and my mother.

In a few days, I went back to the University, and as soon as he was able—in his judgment, not the doctor's—he set a crew to slicking up the church inside and out. And somewhere in there he took time to put the papers in his strongbox in order and write the letter. So he was prepared, even if I was not.

Oh, I was expecting it. I was even ready for it, knew what must be done. But anticipation of loss is a far cry from experiencing it. So when the call came that morning—and I knew with certainty what it was before I even lifted the phone—I was almost overwhelmed.

When Mrs. Theobold had finished telling me, making the point that he had died in his sleep, peacefully and without pain, I gave the orders without even thinking about them.

"Call Malones', but tell them I want him brought back home tonight. And call Sarah and tell her I need her. And tell her to tell Brother Uriah that he's to preach the funeral. You can expect me in four hours if not before." Then it occurred to me that it was her loss, too, and knowing it was inadequate but that she would understand the thought, I asked, "Will you be all right?"

Sarah was there at the door in the chill March wind to meet me when I got there, brought the seventy-five miles from their home by Brother Uriah, who had gone back for the Wednesday evening prayer service at the church he pastored but would return the next day. Though we wrote each other weekly, I had not seen her since Mr. Hayes' first attack when she and Brother Uriah had driven over and spent a day, but time and distance could never really separate us.

Mrs. Theobold was waiting behind her. She had buried a husband and a grown son, and she had kept house for Mr. Hayes and me for twenty-five years and now he was gone, yet she stood like a rock. When I put my arms around her, I could feel the stiffness. But self-sacrifice was bred into her.

"You must be wore out," she said. "I'll get some coffee."

Sarah took my hand and led me into the new living room. She and Mrs. Theobold had already rearranged it. "We will need to put him in here," she said. "I know you would have liked the old room better, but it's small and there will be a big crowd."

She was right. We never used this room. Mr. Hayes had built the store more than half a century ago. Then when he married, he had added living quarters behind it. When New Zion was established and began to boom, he built a new store there and tore down the old one, replacing it with an addition to our living quarters that, from some innate sense of proportion he possessed, came out looking as if it had all been carefully designed and built at the same time. The two front rooms on the ground floor were large and light and formally furnished, one as a living room and the other as a dining room with a wide entry hall between. We used neither of them. We continued to sit in our old living room, where we felt easy, and to eat in the kitchen. I could see that the old living room would not begin to accommodate all those who would want to come. And though it had long since become common practice, I could not accept the idea of having him lie in the funeral home.

Mrs. Theobold brought the coffee, but I decided to have it in the kitchen, so we sat at the table. Then I let Sarah persuade me to lie down. She came with me to my room and held my hand while I closed my eyes and tried to relax. I didn't think I would be able to sleep, but I did and woke to Sarah's light touch on my forehead, unaware that I had slept or of the passage of time.

"He's here," she said.

We went down together. Mrs. Theobold was waiting for us in

the hall. The sliding double doors of both front rooms had been opened and folding chairs had been set up in the dining room to take the overflow.

Sarah had had them place the casket, which she and Mrs. Theobold had chosen earlier, next to the front windows. The lid was raised and draped with a white veil. As we approached, I hesitated, unwilling to see him dead, but the gentle pressure of Sarah's hand on my arm urged me on. She lifted the veil. He looked only asleep, as I had seen him so many times, in his chair or lying on the couch in the long summer afternoons. The three of us looked for a while. Then Sarah dropped the veil.

Mrs. Theobold insisted then that I eat something, arguing, as I knew she would, that I must keep up my strength, so Sarah and I went back to the kitchen, leaving Mrs. Theobold to sit with him, satisfying the old custom that from the time it is laid out until it is buried a corpse must never be left unattended.

Mrs. Theobold's kitchen door had been kept busy with people bringing food. The counter tops were loaded with cakes and pies, and the refrigerator, when Sarah opened it, was filled with cold meats and sandwiches and casseroles and salads. They weren't just for us; those coming would expect to be fed something, and those who would sit through the night would need to be sustained. I had intended just to have some coffee, but the sight of all that food reminded me that I hadn't eaten since morning. Sarah heated some soup, and we each had a cup and a sandwich.

The first ones arrived before we finished.

"Take your time," Sarah said. "Mrs. Theobold will handle it. Besides, it's going to be a long night."

And it was.

I had been through such things with Mr. Hayes dozens of times, but not in the roles we were now playing. There was a ritual to follow. Callers were met near the front door by some member of the family. This position was rotated between Mrs. Theobold and Sarah. After a brief word, the visitors would file by the casket, stopping and taking some time to view the body. Then they would come over to me. I had chosen to stand across the room from the casket and was supported by either Sarah or Mrs. Theobold, depending on which one was keeping station at the door. There was no blood tie among the four of us—Mr. Hayes, Mrs. Theobold, Sarah and myself—yet there was no question that we were a family. Finally, having expressed their condolences, the callers would find seats and converse among themslves. The whole affair was conducted with soft step and whisper as a measure of respect for death.

They came in droves, and at one time were lined up outside waiting to get in. They filled not only the two front rooms but our old living room and the kitchen, and Mrs. Theobold even opened up her little sitting room on the ground floor. They filled the hall stairs from bottom to top, sitting on the steps and almost blocking passage to the upstairs bathrooms. Those who managed to make their way to the kitchen cleaned out most of the food except what had been set aside for those who would stay and watch through the night.

After a while, the faces, though familiar, became a blur to me, and I settled on a few stock responses and repeated them automatically. Finally, around ten-thirty, the crowd began to thin out, and by eleven they were all gone except those who had agreed among themselves to stay the night—Rile Blackburn and Big Jack Heddin and Will and Herman Poser.

I suddenly realized that I was exhausted. I found a chair in the hall and sank into it. I knew that Sarah and Mrs. Theobold must be as tired as I was, but Mrs. Theobold had gone to the kitchen to set out the food for the watchers and Sarah was straightening up. After a while, Mrs. Theobold came back and spoke to the watchers and then came to tell me she was going to bed. When I put my arms around her, the stiffness was still there. Then Sarah came and turned me by the shoulders and headed me toward the stairs. "I'll bring some coffee in a few minutes," she told me.

I stretched out on my bed, but my tiredness was only physical—the long drive, five hours of standing and the other tensions of the day—and I was wide awake. When Sarah came, I was sitting on the side of the bed and had decided. "Let's have it in his room," I said.

She looked startled at first, then smiled and without a word carried the tray to Mr. Hayes' room and set it on the night stand beside the bed. She had brought sandwiches as well as coffee. She plugged the pot into the outlet behind the night stand and filled our cups. "Eat something, too," she said.

I took one of the sandwiches. We sat side by side on the edge of the bed while we ate.

"He foresaw this, you know," Sarah said.

"What!"

"That we would come here, or at least that you would."

Mr. Hayes had always taken great pleasure in trying to predict what others would do and then in amazing them with his foresight. He especially enjoyed showing off to me. And really, he was very good at this game of his. Part of it was logical deduction, part was a highly developed sensitivity to subtle cues and part was pure hunch. And then, too, he was lucky, sometimes phenomenally so. But that he would have known that I would come here on the night of his death, with or without Sarah, was more than I could swallow.

"I had a letter from him two weeks ago," Sarah said, "nothing special in it, just news and gossip, but he added a postscript which didn't make any sense to me. I thought it was just another one of those obscure jokes of his and I had missed the point. It said, 'Remind him the strongbox is under the bed.'"

The laughter started deep inside and shook my whole body. Sarah, watching, took my cup out of my hand before I spilled it. What a long shot! And he had hit it! Against impossible odds!

For in order for it to work out, Sarah had to be here. Well, he could have been pretty well assured of her presence, but not necessarily at the right time. Maybe he remembered, and counted on me to remember, his remark made only once to me that summer twelve years ago when we were first beginning to know her: *If I'm ever down and you can't manage, send for her.* Or our words to each other, Sarah's and mine, in the fall when we parted:

If you ever need me, send for me and I will come.
And what about Uriah?
If you send, I will know you need me more than Uriah.

I had sent for her, the first and only time since she had made that commitment. I had done it automatically and without thought.

But assuming her here, give him that, how could he have counted on her remembering? He had thrown it in as a postscript, not deigning to explain, and she hadn't even understood what he was talking about, had in fact forgotten until my suggestion that we go to his room to have the coffee reminded her. And certainly he could not have counted on, and I really didn't believe even he could have foreseen the possibility of, my being wound up to the point where sleep would be out of the question and at the same time being taken by the need to be somewhere that would evoke his presence.

It was a final grand gesture, the ultimate display of his genius, and the last and longest shot of his life. I wanted to stand up and cheer. I explained to Sarah, and we laughed together.

After a while, I fished under the bed for the strongbox, brought it out and put it on the bed. We sat with our backs against the headboard and went through it.

The first thing we came across was a copy of his will. I had seen it before. It was very simple. It provided a small annuity for Mrs. Theobold and left everything else to me.

Next, we found a thick stack of deeds held together by rubber bands. As we worked our way through them, Sarah remarked that it was like playing Monopoly, and for the first time in my life, I realized what I should have known if I had ever stopped to think about it: Mr. Hayes had been an extremely wealthy man.

Sarah found the picture slipped in among the deeds.

"Who . . . ?" she said. I knew. It was Susan. His beloved Susan. My mother.

"Why, she's beautiful," Sarah said.

The photograph had been shot with a soft focus, and fading had further softened the definition. The vagueness of line probably enhanced her long straight features. I doubt most would have judged her beautiful, but she was not unattractive. Her forehead was high, her eyes well spaced, her lips full. Her chin was strong and had a faint cleft. Her hair was straight and fell over her shoulders and breast.

"He probably kept it here to protect it from the light," Sarah said. She carefully slipped the photograph back into the stack of deeds.

The only other thing in the strongbox was a letter. It was sealed in a plain white envelope without an address. I opened it and we read it together, I aloud and she silently with me.

It began, *Dear Jim and Sarah.* We laughed again at his triumph.

If I am wrong about this, I am going to look like the biggest fool in the world, but it won't matter to me because I will never know it. But if I am right, then you can chalk one up to my credit. I am, of course, assuming that I will be right.

I will go even further and try to lay it all out for you. I will say that you will be reading this before the funeral. If I am right, it will be the night before, the night when my friends will all come to see me. I will be laid out in the front living room, because the other one will not be big enough and you would not use the funeral home. Sometime in there, Sarah will remember to give you my message. It will probably be after things have

*quietened down, after they have all gone except the ones who
will be staying through the night. You will come to my room
and open the strongbox and find the letter. You will both be sitting on my bed as you read it, because I have only the one chair
and you will want to sit together. So the two of you will be sitting there while I talk to you through this letter, and directly
below, one floor down, I will be lying in state so to speak while
three or four of my friends will be sitting with me and no doubt
swapping lies about me. Well, enough of that.*

Enough and to spare! We could not help but be amazed.

*The reason for this letter is that there is something I need to
say that I never got around to before.*

I want to make a confession.

*You were right, along with Rile and Mrs. Blackburn. That
was him they found out there in the old graveyard.*

I closed my eyes and put the letter down. What he was
about to say, I didn't want to hear, didn't want to know. I knew
Mr. Hayes was capable. And there was no question about
provocation. I recognized that the probability that Mr. Hayes
had killed him was very strong. And I knew if I asked him he
would tell me the truth. But that preacher, my father, was
nothing to me. If I had known for certain that Mr. Hayes was
guilty, I think I could have accepted it. But somehow I could
never bring myself to put it to the test. I never confronted him
with it.

Sarah knew nothing of this. It was, I suppose, the only
thing in my life, significant or otherwise, I had not talked to
her about.

I felt her slip the letter from under my fingers. She took up
where I had left off.

But you were wrong in thinking I killed him. I would have, but I didn't get the chance. He took it out of my hands.

I came into the room and found him in bed with her. He was lying face down, half over her, and she was staring at the ceiling. I yelled. He jumped up and tried to get away. I was blocking the door. But it was not me he was trying to get away from. I doubt he was even aware that I was there. His eyes were wild and unfocussed, and he was shouting, Judas! Judas Iscariot! and waving his arms around. One of his hands caught me in the side of the head and knocked me against the door post and stunned me. When I came to myself, he was gone. I went to the living room and took down a pistol and loaded it and went out looking for him.

After a while, I remembered that locust thicket where he would go to pray. That is where I found him. He had hung himself. He had taken the rope off that little mule of his and hung himself.

Sarah fumbled for my hand and squeezed hard, her face registering horror. It was a while before she could continue.

So I caught that little mule and loaded him on it and took him out to the graveyard and buried him. At the time, I just wanted to get him out of my sight, to erase the whole thing. And I didn't say anything because I couldn't bear for anybody to know what he had done to Susan, wanted to forget it myself. But that was not to be.

By the time it became obvious that he was the father, the church had already been established. There were some who wanted to pull away. If I had spoken out then, I think that would have finished the church. You, Jim, will understand why I didn't want that to happen. And I know you, Sarah, will not need to understand to accept that as true.

Maybe I did understand, or now, at least, was beginning to. Sarah had once told me in our early years that I felt responsible for the people of Zions Cause. At the time I had rejected the idea, but through the years I had come to see that she had been right. Not only that, I realized I had caught that sense of responsibility from Mr. Hayes, that duty to see to it, wherever possible, that the mix of justice and mercy which he had called fairness prevailed. Despite the pain the circumstances of the establishment of the church had brought him, Mr. Hayes saw in it an aim which paralleled, perhaps even transcended his own.

I took the letter from Sarah and read on.

When they found him, I should have told it then. It wouldn't have made all that much difference anymore. The church was no longer vulnerable. And by that time, I had long since forgiven him, realized that it was not an act of volition and that some of the responsibility was mine. But when I saw I could win out over Rile and Mrs. Blackburn, I thought I would just let it lie. Habit, I guess. But then you claimed the cross, and I knew you knew it was him. I knew, too, that you would take the next step and ask yourself how he got there and that would lead you to me.

And here is the confession. Through all these years I have deliberately let you go on thinking that I killed him. My motive, I am sorry to say, was pure vanity. You knew that if you asked I would have told you the truth. But I knew that you would not ask unless you were certain that, whatever the answer, you could accept it. The act of your asking was the test, the proof I needed, or thought I needed, of the strength of your love for me. I realize now the selfishness of that test and the vanity that inspired it and, above all, the foolishness of needing to test something that our years together should have made obvious and beyond question. So, there it is, Jim. I am truly sorry for my sin against you. Knowing you, I know that you will already have forgiven me. But confession is for the benefit of the sinner, not the sinned against.

Be that as it may, I knew I had shucked off a heavy load, one that I had carried so long I had grown used to its weight and only now that it was gone realized how really burdensome it had been.

Just a couple of things more, and then I am done. First, about this impossible love affair of yours.

Sarah and I exchanged a smile. Impossible was right, everything about it. Even so, it had endured twelve years and was still going strong.

I have never tried to interfere before. I do so now knowing that the chances of me changing your mind are pretty slim. But I also recognize that the circumstances give me a certain advantage, and I hope you will forgive me but I am about to exercise it.

What I want to say is this: Don't deny yourselves forever. I know about denial, but I had no choice. You do. You chose to take the punishment. But there has been punishment enough. Choose now to end it. Don't waste what surely must be the most precious thing on earth. Or in heaven, too, for that matter. Oh, what I would give, even now, for one brief moment with Susan!

I could not go on. Even if I could have seen the words on the page, my voice would have failed me. I felt Sarah's cheek, wet against mine, and we sat there clinging to each other.

After a time, she slipped away from me and got up. She closed the strongbox and slid it back under the bed, put the letter on the night stand and turned out the light. We undressed, got into bed, loved and slept, holding each other through the night.

In the morning we finished the letter. There wasn't much more.

About the church. Don't try to hang on to it for my sake. Once the funeral is over, let that be it. It will be a good stopping place. The first funeral held there was Susan's. Let mine be the last. That will round things off nicely.

Well, that about does it. That is all I had in mind to say, except

Love to you both,

Jim Hayes

P.S. Don't forget to straighten the bed. Mrs. Theobold would be scandalized.

"He is absolutely . . . ," Sarah said, stopping to search for a word, "absolutely incredible!"

"And also incorrigible," I said.

Through the window I could see the first blush of sunrise across the lake. It promised a fair day for the funeral. I would miss him for the rest of my life. But I was done with grief.